"Why are you not in bed, *signorina*?"

The tone of his voice was somehow accusing.

"Something woke me up," Helen said. "I thought I saw a woman." In her mind the shadowy figure was growing less distinct and Helen shook her head in confusion. "It frightened me."

Guido turned her toward her bedroom. "If you are fearful that someone is in your room, I will reassure you." He slipped past her and turned on the lights. The room was, of course, empty.

Helen's voice was husky as she thanked him for his trouble. Looking up, she lost herself in the gleaming depths of his black eyes.

He slid his hand around her waist and drew her toward him. His touch fired her senses and she couldn't move away....

The Tears of Venus

by

REBECCA STRATTON

Harlequin Books

TORONTO • LONDON • NEW YORK • AMSTERDAM
SYDNEY • HAMBURG • PARIS • STOCKHOLM

Original hardcover edition published in 1979
by Mills & Boon Limited

ISBN 0-373-02339-1

Harlequin edition published June 1980

Printed in U.S.A.

CHAPTER ONE

THE long twisting road wound ever higher into the Tuscan hills, and to Helen it was beginning to seem endless, even though the countryside was breathtaking and she was quite enchanted by it. Dust whirled thickly from the stony surface that crackled under the wheels of the car, and the sunlight made dark glasses imperative, but there was a fresh beauty in the scenery that found a response in her emotions and increased the sense of anticipation she felt as they came ever nearer their destination.

Orchards and vineyards stretched out in slumbrous fertility over the hillsides, bound inextricably together by the twisting ribbon of road and broken here and there by dazzling white villas. Homes built in the cool of the hills above the town, and behind high walls, set amid an extravagance of jasmine, clematis and mimosa. A light wind stirred the paintbrush tops of dark cypress trees, brushing an azure sky with light strokes of thin white cloud, and Helen thought of the bliss of living in such a setting.

It was much more exotic than she had imagined even, and the air smelled of the mingled scents of flowers and trees, inextricably mixed with the aridity of heat and dust. Her face flushed by the stuffiness of the car, she glanced at her companion, and wondered how he was feeling. But Vincenzo was coming home; she was coming to a whole new world.

She had not known Vincenzo Alessio very long and the thought uppermost in her mind as she glanced at him again was the same that had niggled her on and off ever since they left London. She wished she was more sure of the situation that awaited her, for it had all happened in such a hurry and she felt she should have taken more time to think about what might be in store for her.

It was true that she had needed to find herself another job, and certainly the prospect of working in Italy had more appeal than a post in a suburban English school, but she had only Vincenzo's word that his family were ready to accept her as readily as he claimed. Vincenzo was susceptible, no one could deny it, and Helen was too discerning not to recognise her own attractions. He had been impressed, but she was concerned that his emotions might have influenced his judgment and made him too optimistic.

At the time they met she had been employed by some English friends of his as a temporary nursemaid for their small daughter, although she had in fact recently qualified as a teacher. It had been when her employer expressed regret at losing her, now that the little girl was to go to school, that Vincenzo had come up with a solution to her redundancy.

His eldest brother, he said, was in need of someone as tutor-companion for his daughter, an older girl than her present charge, but just as charming. Helen was, he insisted, just the type of young woman that was required; a qualified teacher and obviously very fond of children. She was ideal from every point of view; and he had obviously included his own.

All the arrangements had been made by Vincenzo, the only thing required of her being her consent to the move, and that she had given willingly. It was only later that she realised how very much a pig-in-a-poke arrangement it was, for both her and her new employer. She knew very little about him, and he virtually nothing about her, so that she wondered what kind of a man would engage the services of a complete stranger to care for his daughter; and a foreigner, what was more.

She glanced again at the face of the man beside her and could not help liking what she saw; if Guido Alessio was half as handsome and charming as his brother, she felt there was little to worry about. Vincenzo was a few years older than she was, about twenty-five or six, she guessed, and darkly good-looking in the Latin tradition. His eyes were dark and put her in mind of brown velvet, and he had thick black hair above a smooth classical brow. His mouth was somewhat full and frankly sensual and he smiled a great deal. Seeming never in doubt of his own charm, his manner nevertheless suggested confidence rather than mere brashness, and Helen found him alarmingly attractive.

From the very first evening he had singled her out, when she had been helping out at a dinner party her employers were giving, and after that he had sought her company at every available opportunity. Helen had never suffered from false modesty concerning her own looks, but Vincenzo Alessio had made more impression on her susceptible nature than anyone had ever done before, and she enjoyed his lavish compliments unashamedly.

Her face was heart-shaped and owed its soft beauty as much to an inner warmth as to physical perfection. Golden-fair hair curled a little at the nape of her neck and around her ears, and a suggestion of a fringe wisped across her brow above eyes that were, rather unexpectedly with such Saxon fairness, a definite hazel. Glinting with tawny lights when she smiled, and set between thick brown lashes. At present they were hidden behind dark glasses, but Vincenzo must have sensed her looking at him, and he half-turned his head for a moment, showing his almost too perfect teeth in a dazzling smile.

'You like it, eh?' he asked, indicating the surrounding countryside with an expressive hand, then went on without waiting for an answer. 'You will like Tuscany very much, Helen, and you will like us too, I am sure of it.' Confident dark eyes smiled at her for a second before turning their attention back to the road. 'You already like me, *si*?'

'Yes, of course.' She returned his smile, though rather less confidently, for they could not be far from their destination now, and she was thankful for the dark glasses that hid the uncertainty she felt must show in her eyes. 'I shouldn't be here if I didn't like you, Vincenzo, but it's rather more important that your family, and your brother in particular, likes *me*, if I'm to work for him.'

Vincenzo shrugged his elegantly clad shoulders with what she suspected was assumed carelessness, and his handsome features were distorted for a moment by a grimace. 'Ah, *si*; but you will not need to see very much of Guido, and you will not let him—scare you off, eh?'

It was a suggestion not guaranteed to boost her courage, and Helen eyed him for a moment, frowning slightly. 'Will he try to scare me off?' she asked, and quite unconsciously tightened the grip she had on her handbag. 'Why should I be scared off, Vincenzo? Is your brother likely to take exception to me?'

'No, of course he will not!' He reached out and squeezed her hands, but his palm felt moist and Helen could not help wondering if it might be nerves and not simply the heat that made it so. 'He is always so busy with his horses that he will not trouble himself much with anything else. He is one of the top show-jumpers in the world, you know, and that means that he is constantly keeping his horses and himself in top form for the big shows. He works very hard to stay where he is, although soon now——'

He left the rest unspoken, letting a shrug complete

his meaning. Very obviously Vincenzo was very proud of his brother's achievements, and with cause; even she had heard of Guido Alessio, and she was no particular fan of the sport. Any major event in the world of show-jumping was almost bound to feature him among the winners, and it had been her previous employers' enthusiasm for his reputation that had been the basis of Vincenzo's friendship with them. And had indirectly been responsible for his meeting with Helen.

'You will be very happy with us,' Vincenzo assured her, 'and you will adore Isabella, just as she will adore you.'

More than once Helen had been tempted to ask whether his brother was widowed or divorced, or simply living apart from his wife, but she had never yet got around to it. It seemed rather too much like prying somehow, and she reasoned that if it was something Vincenzo wanted her to know he would tell her in his own time. Nevertheless she ventured to bring the rather unconventional circumstances of her engagement to his notice, and remind him of how chancy the whole situation was in fact.

'It's all very much a case of taking pot-luck,' she pointed out. 'I can't help thinking, Vincenzo, that I should have made some sort of contact with your brother before I committed myself, or before having your brother commit *him*self. He is, after all, employing me to care for his daughter purely on your say-so; he must be very trusting.'

'He is practical,' Vincenzo said, dispensing with the idea of his brother's trust in him. 'Guido knows I would not be foolish enough to recommend anyone unsuitable. He knows also that I would not bring anyone who was not going to love *mia bella* Isabella as I do.'

Helen glanced at him curiously. She had heard that the Italians treasured their children, but Vincenzo's manner always suggested that he doted on his young niece, and it was not the kind of thing she would have credited him with. 'You think a lot of her, don't you?' she ventured, and Vincenzo gave her a swift, darting glance from the corners of his eyes before he nodded.

'But of course,' he agreed. 'We all think a great deal of Isabella, she is a very charming and delightful *bambina*, as you will soon discover.'

'How soon?' she asked, but knew from the way he glanced every so often at the glimpses of white walls through the trees ahead that it would only be as long as it took him to drive them there.

In confirmation he waved a hand at the tantalising flashes of dazzling white that fluttered among the dark cypress. 'Just a few moments now,' he promised, and turned to smile at her as he drove the car in through an arched gateway. His dark eyes scanned her slightly flushed face below gleaming gold hair, and he smiled again. 'I think they will be pleased with my choice,' he said and, a few seconds later, '*Benvenuto*, Helen!'

Like almost everything he did, Vincenzo's formal welcome to his home was made with a flourish, using one long slim hand to take in a wide half-circle of stone-paved driveway in front of the villa as they swept round on to it from the approach. He applied the brake and brought the car to a halt, pressing the horn in the same moment so that its raucous summons shattered the sudden quiet before Helen had time to accustom her ears to it.

'Come!'

He was out of his own seat and standing beside her with the car door open, waiting for her to join him, but at the same time his head was half turned to look over his shoulder at the door that stood partly open. As if he was expecting to see someone, Helen felt. He slid a hand under her arm as she got out, and stood for a moment to give her time to look at the villa before they went in.

It was charming and, just as Helen had hoped, very like the other homes they had passed on their way there. Two stories high and built of the local stone, it was dazzlingly white in the brilliant sunshine and sprawled lazily amid its surrounding mass of blooms. It seemed to be free of ugly angles, although obviously they were there somewhere beneath the mass of climbing shrubs that softened the outline and reflected soft colours in the quartz-bright stone. It struck Helen as quite breathtakingly lovely, and her expression showed how she felt, obviously to Vincenzo's satisfaction.

'You like it?'

She nodded without hesitation. 'It's beautiful,' she said, and Vincenzo laughed, squeezing his fingers into her arm as he urged her towards the house and the half-open door.

'Come!' He repeated that rather anxious encouragement, and Helen obeyed automatically.

Inside, the villa was more home-like than she anticipated, after having seen the exotic exterior, but it was luxurious nevertheless and just as attractive as the outside. The walls were covered with a light blue paper with an embossed design and gilded at ceiling level with a frieze of leaves and flowers, soft and cool looking in the more subdued light. It was bright and airy, and the floor showed a tiled mosaic of blue, green and white rather stylised flowers and leaves around the edge of a deep blue carpet.

A blue glass vase of immense proportions stood at the foot of the staircase, filled with branches of fresh blooms from the garden, and the staircase itself curved away upward in a graceful sweep of shallow treads and white-painted balustrades. Its very splendid impression was brought cosily down to earth by the sight of a child's summer coat hung carelessly over the newel post, with one of its sleeves turned inside out.

'Isabella! Hey, Isabella, *dov'è*, eh?'

Vincenzo called at the top of his voice, then swung round with a laugh when a door opened and a little girl came running out, hurling herself into his arms. He lifted her and swung her round while the two of them laughed loudly in unison, and Helen smiled indulgently, a little apart. Breathless, he put the child back on her feet and she could see the subtle likenesses in what were at first glance two quite different faces.

Isabella Alessio was ten years old, that much Helen knew about her new charge, but even Vincenzo's avuncular enthusiasm had not done justice to her prettiness, and she stood beside him, looking at Helen with huge dark eyes. There was a cameo classicism about the small, almost perfect features, and yet they showed a shy friendliness that was both charming and appealing.

Quite surprisingly, to Helen, her skin was fair and had a suggestion of freckles, and her long hair was light brown, not black like her uncle's. In fact apart from those enormous and very dark eyes she could have more easily passed for English rather than Italian, and Helen was once again made curious about the identity of her mother.

Taking her hand, Vincenzo turned back to Helen, his eyes gleaming and warm with pleasure as he introduced them. 'Helen, I would like you to meet Isabella. Isabella, *polla mia*, this is Signorina Purvis who has come to take the place of Signora Billings.' He indicated the carelessly abandoned coat. 'And none too soon it appears, huh? Do we now drape the *balaustrata* with our clothes, *piccola*?'

Far from being cowed by his reprimand, the child rolled her huge eyes mischievously before offering her hand to Helen. 'How do you do, Signorina Purvis,' she said, in such excellent English that Helen heaved an inward sigh of relief. 'I am sorry about not putting away my coat, but'—the shrug of her thin shoulders was pure Italian—'I forgot about it because I was so happy to think about Tio Vincenzo coming home.'

She was a charmer too, Helen realised, seeing the effect of such blatant flattery on Vincenzo. Clasping the small warm hand in hers, Helen smiled. 'How do you do, Isabella.' She met the warm friendly eyes directly, determined to start off on the right foot. 'I'm very relieved to find that your uncle didn't exaggerate when he said you spoke very good English. I don't know if your father knows that I don't speak any Italian; did Vin—your uncle tell him that?'

Isabella gave him a bright mischievous glance when she noticed the slip, as if she read all kinds of meaning into it, and she was obviously gratified by Helen's praise of her English. 'It does not matter, *signorina*,' she assured her. 'My teacher, Signora Billings, always spoke to me in English. I have spoken it always, since I was very small.'

Why? Helen wondered. Why was it necessary for an Italian child, living in Italy, always to speak English in the schoolroom, and to have an English governess? She had no idea of the answer at the moment, and it was not really important as long as she was not expected to know any Italian.

'I hope you are not annoyed about my coat,' Isabella said, although the bright eager look in her eyes scarcely suggested she would be very upset about it if Helen was annoyed. She was a bright, sunny child, and seemingly well brought up, but she was quite used to her own way, Helen guessed, and thought her Uncle Vincenzo probably did as much of the spoiling as anyone.

'I'm not annoyed,' Helen assured her, glancing across at the offending garment once more. 'But I should hang it up somewhere if I were you before it loses its shape. It looks rather a nice one, and it would be a shame to spoil it.'

'When I go upstairs to change my clothes,' Isabella promised, quite amenable to correction, apparently. Then she added, as if it mattered more than Helen's opinion, 'Papà will not be home yet.'

That aroused speculation about just how strictly Guido Alessio was bringing up his daughter, and yet again Helen realised how very little she knew about the people she was to live and work with from now on. She would have preferred to meet her new employer right away, but if what Isabella said was true, he would not be arriving home until later.

'Signor Alessio isn't here now?' she asked, and Vincenzo looked at her and smiled as he shook his head.

'Not right at this moment,' he told her. 'But do not worry, Helen, you will meet your new boss soon enough. In the meantime I will take you to meet the rest of our family. Eh, Isabella?'

He addressed himself to his niece, and the girl took his hand looking up at him and smiling. 'I shall like Signorina Purvis very much, Tio Vincenzo,' she told him, and he hugged her close for a second.

'I think you will too, *piccola*,' he said, then turned and pulled Helen into the curve of his other arm. 'So shall I!'

They walked all together across the hall, and Isabella looked up at her uncle's smoothly handsome face with a gleam of mischief in her eyes. 'The *signorina* is very beautiful, Tio Vincenzo, yes? Not—ordinary as Signora Billings was. Did you not say——'

'I said that you chatter too much,' Vincenzo told her, kissing the soft childish face affectionately. 'And it seems that I was right, huh? Maybe Signorina Purvis will not stay with such a chatterer.'

But Isabella's smile was confident. There was a curiously adult knowingness in her expression that made Helen slightly uneasy. It was almost as if she had her own ideas why Helen was there and why her uncle had recommended her. She glanced from her uncle to Helen, peering around him to do so, and she smiled.

'Of course the *signorina* will stay,' she assured him confidently, and it seemed that Vincenzo shared her confidence, for he winked an eye at her.

The room they walked into was big and cool, and both comfortable and luxurious. Beige walls took on a faintly greenish tint from the filtered light from half-shuttered windows, the carpet underfoot matching exactly, even to the tint of green. Paintings hung at intervals on the walls, soft misty landscapes for the most part, but one or two portraits as well that could have been family ancestors, by their features. Those classically handsome faces with slightly insolent eyes and sensual mouths were very like Vincenzo's.

There were already two women and a man in the room when they went in, and Isabella turned to take Vincenzo's hand in hers, pulling him along after her like a triumphant captor and smiling broadly. The man got to his feet the moment they came in, and Helen was conscious of being the target of three pairs of eyes that followed her progress across the room, linked inescapably with Vincenzo's arm through hers.

Vincenzo was smiling too; confident of his own welcome and of hers too, apparently not for a moment realising how precipitate he was being by introducing a future employee into the family circle as if she was a guest. The other man was only a little older than Vincenzo, she guessed, and so much like him to look at that it was easy to assume he was the middle brother, Pietro.

From the way he looked at her it was clear that he shared Vincenzo's appreciation of feminine beauty too, but bowing to good form, he took a back seat for the moment while she was introduced to the ladies. The elder of the two was about forty-five years old, lean and dark and with black eyes that regarded her flatly, in a way guaranteed to remind her of her lowly status.

Helen felt a curious chilling sensation as she stood in front of her, but she had little difficulty guessing her identity.

'Tia Olivia,' said Vincenzo, smiling in the face of discouragement, 'I would like to introduce Signorina Purvis who is to take the place of Signora Billings. Helen, this is my aunt, Signorina Alessio. Helen speaks no Italian, Tia Olivia,' he added, 'but your English is very good, is it not?'

Helen recalled the face Vincenzo had made when he told her about his father's unmarried sister, and it seemed that Olivia Alessio was going to live up to her reputation. She extended a thin hand but made no attempt to clasp Helen's, and she gave her a long, hard look while she murmured a brief greeting in English.

The scrutiny complete, she switched her hard black eyes back to her nephew and frowned, and when she spoke again it was in Italian, with the obvious intention of passing an opinion that was unintelligible to Helen. For the first time since she had known him, Helen saw Vincenzo grow angry, and the change in his handsome features was startling for a moment. His recovery was rapid, however, and when he answered his aunt it was in English; clear, precise and very deliberate.

'Helen is also a very good friend of mine, Tia Olivia,' he said, 'and I shall expect her to be treated with the courtesy due to her.'

'Is Guido aware of this—friendship?' his aunt enquired in her flat, thin voice, and for a moment Vincenzo looked vaguely discomfited.

'Helen is everything I claimed her to be,' he said. 'Guido will have no cause for complaint.' With that he turned away from her and smiled with his customary charm at the younger woman, bending first to kiss her on both cheeks before he introduced her. 'Bianca, carissima, this is Helen Purvis. Helen, my sister-in-law

Bianca, and beside her, the man with the wild and roving eye, is my brother Pietro.'

Clearly the two men were on the best of terms, and as far as Helen could see Bianca Alessio took no heed of the reference to her handsome husband's obviously appreciative eye. From Vincenzo, Helen knew that his aunt had not approved of Pietro's choice of a wife, that he had married her rather than the wealthy heiress that Olivia Alessio had preferred for him.

At first sight it was difficult to see what had attracted a man like Pietro to such a quiet and very ordinary young woman, but quite clearly he loved her, for it showed in the way he smiled and placed a gentle hand on her shoulder as Vincenzo introduced her. A small but touchingly protective gesture that spoke volumes.

Bianca was about twenty-six, Helen guessed; a plump, dark girl with gentle eyes and a slightly hesitant manner when she shook hands. She appeared to be about six or seven months pregnant and not bearing up very well, for her skin had an unhealthy pallor and her eyes, for all their gentleness, lacked lustre. She murmured her greeting in strongly accented English, then immediately looked up at her husband as if seeking his approval.

Pietro Alessio made up for his wife's reticence by being as extrovertly confident as his brother. He took her proffered hand and first shook it in the conventional way, then turned it over his own and bent to kiss her fingers, a mere light touch with his lips that was to Helen quite alarmingly affecting. He too had those deep, soft velvet-brown eyes, like Vincenzo, and he smiled at her charmingly.

'You are most welcome, Miss Purvis,' he told her. 'I am sure that you will enjoy being with us, and you are already enchanted with our little Isabella, I think?'

Helen was given no opportunity to express her agreement, before her new charge spoke up for herself, in no doubt of her own feelings. 'I like the *signorina* very much, Tio Pietro,' she told him. 'And so does Tio Vincenzo.'

The last part of her declaration brought laughter from both her uncles, and only Olivia Alessio, sitting stern and disapproving in her armchair, showed quite plainly that the appointment did not have unqualified approval. 'Will it not be as well to wait and discover whether Guido is of the same opinion?' she asked in her prim voice, and in a moment of sudden apprehension, Helen could only agree with her.

Helen had been given a room next to that of her charge, and the comfort and luxury of it took her breath away. She had never even dreamed of living in such surroundings, and she had difficulty even now actually believing it was true and not some wild fancy she was dreaming. She had spent some time just walking around the bedroom and bathroom, proving to herself that it really was as incredible as it seemed. And that she really could bathe in a green marble bath surrounded by white and gold walls, and a huge gilt-framed mirror that reflected her warm nakedness through an erotic mist of steam.

The bedroom was huge, and indulged the senses with deep fur rugs and silk coverlets, with heavy damask curtains and the scent of roses fluttering crimson heads against the half-open shutters. The windows were tall, virtually floor to ceiling, and looked out across the gardens at the back of the villa.

She could look from there down a sloping hillside to a small town in the distance that looked dazzlingly white in the sunlight, and between, to the sprawling abundance of vineyards and olive groves. The vines were heavy with grapes, thrusting up through the dry stony soil that stirred dustily in a light wind, and the olives staggered in their grey, twisted rows off into the distance, the whole scene warmed by the late August sun at its most mellow.

By leaning a little out of the window, Helen discovered, she could see a row of low-built, white stables fringed around with cypress trees and facing on to a white fenced paddock with what appeared to be a full-sized jumping arena complete with fences. It was deserted at the moment, but the sight of it reminded her that she had yet to meet her employer, and gain his approval if she was to make a success of her new post. Something in the way his family spoke of him made her wonder if, unlike his two brothers, Guido Alessio resembled their formidable aunt more closely than either of them did, and the thought troubled her more than she cared to admit.

She snatched herself back to reality when she realised the time, and gave a last and rather doubtful look at the pale blue semi-evening dress she had chosen for her first meal with the family. She had little that was really suitable for such grand surroundings, but she felt the blue dress would pass for either a formal or an informal occasion, and she was uncertain which this first dinner would prove to be.

The floating softness of chiffon swirled about her slender legs as she crossed the bedroom, and momentarily boosted her confidence, because it made her feel good. And she was smiling when she walked out on to the carpeted gallery and turned to close the door behind her. It was, after all, too late to regret anything now, and maybe Guido Alessio would prove just as charming and friendly as his two brothers.

The gallery seemed to extend to the whole width of the villa, and a staggering number of rooms opened off its narrow length. The walls were painted white and the rather sparse daylight from high windows, overpowered by artificial light from small glass-shaded lamps placed at intervals, gave the impression of per-

manent night. Tall glass vases of flowers took away any
suggestion of starkness and filled the warm air with
their fragrance, so that Helen paused occasionally on
her way to the stairs to inhale the gorgeous scents of
roses and carnations.

An offer to accompany Isabella downstairs had been
kindly but firmly refused because, so her charge informed her, she meant to go down very early and talk
with Tio Vincenzo. Since she suspected that her own
arrival was one of the subjects to be discussed with her
uncle, Helen accepted the situation and made her own
way down.

The descent of that very grand staircase gave her a
sense of occasion, but it also made her feel rather self-
conscious, especially when she realised that she was not
absolutely sure which was the door of the *salotto*.
Without Isabella's guidance she would have to decide
when she reached the hall which way she should go; in
the meantime she took advantage of the situation and
looked around her with interest.

Paintings hung on the walls of the staircase and it
was only when she looked up at them in passing that
she realised just how big they were. Vast gilt-framed
landscapes that glowed with rich colours and the
mellowness of Italian sunshine: a ripe, lush landscape
that had changed but little with the centuries, she
guessed.

As well as the paintings a large Venetian mirror hung
about halfway down the stairs, and as much to give
herself time to think as to admire her reflection, Helen
paused in front of it. Her face was slightly flushed, she
noted as she stood in the middle of the wide staircase,
gazing at her reflection but also taking note of the
doors reflected in the mirror behind her.

The blue dress suited her, as Vincenzo had said on
another occasion, and she smoothed it down over her
slender shape absently, wishing he would put in an

appearance now and settle the problem of which door to use. The thought had scarcely entered her head when she caught a glimpse of movement from the corner of her eye and turned swiftly, hoping to see Vincenzo.

But she had no need to guess who the man was who came down the wide staircase from the gallery, although his looks came as something of a shock to her after the stunning handsomeness of Vincenzo and Pietro. He must be Guido Alessio. Newspaper photographs of him always showed him in action, crouched over the neck of his mount as the animal took one of the terrifyingly high jumps in competition. They gave little idea of the man himself, and Helen found herself quite inexplicably affected by his appearance.

He was as tall as Vincenzo, perhaps even a little taller, but he had none of the classical, cameo-like handsomeness she expected. Instead his face more nearly resembled the imperious and slightly cruel features of a Roman conqueror, and showed no hint of softness or indolence. The only similarity with his brothers that she could detect in that first startled glance was in the sensual fullness of the lower lip and the bold insolence of the dark eyes. Not velvet-brown in his case, but a bright gleaming black that glittered at her between short thick lashes.

He wore a dark grey suit, expertly tailored to a long lean body, and a white silk shirt and grey tie gave a veneer of civilisation to an otherwise stunningly primitive male. He was long-legged and muscular and walked with the pantherish grace of a big cat, and he held her startled gaze boldly while he came down the stairs towards her. He did not smile, but a glimmer of something lurked for a moment in the black eyes, and could have been amusement.

When she stepped back against the wall, Helen did so quite unconsciously, pressing her hands against the cool smoothness of the mirror as he drew level with her.

The slight backward tilt of her head tipped her hair back from her face with its shadowed hazel eyes and flushed cheeks.

He took stock of her with a lack of inhibition that set her pulse racing so hard her head throbbed with it, then he barely inclined his head in a suggestion of a bow. 'You will be Signorina Purvis, yes?'

His voice was deep, attractive and scarcely accented and it was an automatic reaction when Helen angled her chin a fraction more when she answered him. 'Yes, I am,' she acknowledged. 'Good evening, Mr—Signor Alessio.'

He glanced at the mirror behind her, and one black brow elevated briefly. 'Were you on your way downstairs, *signorina*, or returning to your room? You were halfway, looking at your reflection,' he pointed out when she blinked at him in confusion. 'Perhaps you were dissatisfied with what you saw there?'

Unaccustomed to feeling at a loss, Helen shook her head. 'I—I wasn't sure what I should wear,' she confessed with a frankness born of an unfamiliar nervousness. 'And I don't think I know which door is the right one. I mean,' she added with breathless haste, 'I can't quite remember which one is the *salotto*, there are so many of them.'

He eyed her steadily and she wondered if he suspected that her nervousness might simply be affectation. Eventually, however, he inclined his head in a slightly mocking half-bow, and spread one hand in front of him, palm upwards. 'Permit me to put your mind at rest on both counts, Signorina Purvis,' he said. 'The dress is perfectly suitable, and I shall, with your permission, see that you do not become lost, by escorting you to the *salotto* myself.'

There was nothing to suggest that he was mocking her, and yet Helen found him oddly disturbing. He was more blatantly male than any man she'd ever met before, and he seemed to flaunt his masculinity like a badge of honour with every arrogant gesture he made. He was not immune to her sex, Helen guessed, but gave the impression that he would consider women fair game and there for the taking, with no question of whether or not they were willing.

'Thank you.'

She thankfully accepted his offer to accompany her, and as she walked down the stairs with him she had the opportunity to study him more closely from the corner of her eye. High cheekbones slimmed down to a firm and deeply cleft chin and the clearly defined mouth still had that hint of cruelty, even on closer inspection, the nose bold and aquiline.

While they were crossing the hall he turned his head suddenly and caught her studying him, a black brow swiftly arched so that she immediately looked away. Feeling rather foolishly naïve because she had been so obviously impressed, she felt herself colouring slightly, and at the same time feeling slightly breathless.

'You have met Isabella?' he asked, and Helen answered unhesitatingly.

'Oh yes, and we took to one another right away. I think she's delightful.'

Helen thought he smiled, but she did not look to see how right she was. 'She is also an Alessio,' Guido Alessio reminded her, 'and consequently what you in your country term a bit of a handful, yes? I hope you will not be so beguiled by her that you are lax in your duty, *signorina.*'

Helen, whose methods leaned more towards persuasion than coercion, glanced up at him and frowned. 'You mean you expect me to be strict with her?' she asked, and believed her own feelings were left in no doubt.

'I mean that I wish you to be firm but gentle, *signorina.* I am not a harsh parent, as you probably believe, judging by your expression, but I know Isabella very well and she is charming and delightful, as you say. But like my brothers, she is very skilled at getting her own way, and she is not always amenable to discipline.'

It was something of a family trait, Helen guessed, and could not resist the allusion she made. 'Like her father?' she suggested, and half expected a furious denial; it was after all rather a rash statement.

Instead he answered her quietly and in such a way that she felt horribly childish herself. 'If you wish to make such comparisons, *signorina*—exactly like her father.'

He was opening the door of the *salotto* while he spoke, and brushing quite close against him as she was obliged to, Helen felt the quivering response of her flesh when her bare arm came into contact with him. Glancing up instinctively to murmur her thanks, she met the glowing blackness of his eyes head-on and hastily looked away again, slipping thankfully from his side when she spotted Vincenzo.

'*Cara!*' He had been engaged in a very serious discussion with Isabella, but he drew her into his embrace and stood with an arm about her shoulders while Isabella smiled up at them both with obvious pleasure. 'I will get you a drink, *carina*, wait for me, hah?'

He kissed her cheek lightly before he left her, and when she turned her head Helen noticed Guido Alessio watching her with his black brows drawn, a tight look about his mouth. Her employer, she feared, was going to prove far more like his stern and disapproving aunt than like his handsome and friendly brothers, and as she stood waiting for Vincenzo to bring her a drink, she wondered how she was going to cope. Or even if she could cope at all, for Guido was something quite new in her experience, and she found him much too disturbing.

CHAPTER TWO

HELEN was awake much earlier than usual, her first morning at the Villa Alessio, and rather than lie restlessly abed she got up. It wasn't too early for someone to be about, though probably only the household staff were around so far, and setting foot outside her door seemed to confirm the guess. All the doors along the narrow, quiet gallery were closed, and as far as she could tell no one was stirring as yet.

A hasty peep into Isabella's room had surprised the young occupant in the act of waking, and a smiling enquiry elicited the fact that the girl was quite capable of getting herself up. Taking her at her word, Helen followed her own inclination to be outdoors and she swiftly went through a mental picture of the villa's layout as she approached the stairs.

She was quite sure she could not have found her way around the house itself, but she was pretty confident she could find her way to the front door and out into the garden, and it would be delightfully fresh and cool outside. The lushness of shrubs and flowers would be at their best at this hour of the day and she anticipated their mingled scents and colours as she came downstairs. Luscious, as Vincenzo had said last night when they took a turn around the garden together before going to bed.

Although it was quiet, she was conscious of a curious air of wakefulness that suggested there were other people around somewhere, and as she reached the foot of the stairs and came down into the hall, she caught the faint murmur of voices from somewhere in the rear of the house. She turned her head automatically and smiled to herself when a flurry of Italian ended suddenly in laughter, and she was still smiling when a door opened across on the other side of the hall. Again the turn of her head in the direction of the sound was instinctive.

Guido Alessio was closing the *salotto* door behind him, and Helen told herself that it was only to be expected he would be up and about before the rest of his family. That lean vigorous body was not kept in top physical condition by pampering indulgences like lying in bed of a morning. He didn't notice her at first and she had time to register the fact that he looked just as attractive this morning, dressed for riding, as he had in an expensively formal suit last night.

The imperiously bold profile was just as impressive and the arrogant carriage in no way diminished by more down-to-earth garb. Fawn cord trousers hugged his narrow hips and long legs and with them he wore short, soft leather boots. Against the snowy whiteness of his shirt his black head showed in stunning contrast, and as well as a riding cane he carried a pair of soft leather gloves in one hand.

Glancing up suddenly, he saw her, and stood with one hand still on the door handle looking across at her with his black brows sketching a query. Then he came over to join her, his firm tread muted while he crossed the central area of carpet. 'Good morning, *signorina*,' he said. 'Is something wrong?'

'Wrong?' Just for a moment Helen failed to understand him, then she realised he was merely questioning her early appearance, and she smiled and shook her head. 'Oh no, nothing's wrong, Signor Alessio. I simply felt like a walk before breakfast, that's all.'

'So?'

It was difficult to suppress the sudden more rapid beat of her pulse, and Helen wished he need not look quite so discouragingly stern, for she saw no reason for his apparent disapproval of her. Even her explanation had done nothing to soften the severity of his expression, and he was still regarding her as if he had it in mind to question her motive for taking an early morning walk.

'Is it a regular habit of yours?' he asked, and Helen wondered if he saw such activity at the beginning of the day as a drawback in his daughter's tutor. 'Do you always walk in the mornings when you are at home in England?'

Helen shrugged. He made her uneasy, though she was unwilling to admit it or to let him see that she was. 'Not very often,' she told him. 'But this is new ground for me, and it's such a lovely morning.'

'Isabella is not awake yet?'

The change of subject took her briefly off balance, but she hastily gathered her wits about her, and shook her head. It occurred to her that it might be his way of reminding her of her duty to her charge, and she wanted to put him right about it straight away. 'I looked in on her before I came downstairs,' she explained, and smiled faintly at the recollection. 'She was just waking up and it was made quite clear to me that Isabella needed no assistance in getting herself bathed and dressed. I rather gathered that the suggestion that she did was an affront to her dignity, so I left her to it.'

'It is not part of your duty to help her in that way,' he told her. 'Giustina takes care of her other needs, you are merely required to be her governess. She was not insolent?' he added, and there was a hint of sharpness in his voice that made Helen hasten to qualify any wrong impression she might have given.

'Oh, good heavens, no! But it was obvious that I wasn't needed, so I came for my walk as I wanted to. The gardens are so beautiful, and so is the countryside around here, I can't wait to see more of it. I'm thrilled with everything I've seen so far, though that isn't very much.' A laugh rippled uneasily as she glanced up at that determinedly sober face. 'Vincenzo's brand of driving doesn't give you much time to appreciate the scenery, but what I've seen, I've found enchanting. I suppose that sounds naïve to you,' she suggested, and the angle of her chin challenged him to deny that that was his private opinion, 'but I've never been to Italy before, and it's all so much—more than I expected.'

She was talking far too much and far too fast, but there was something about this man that demolished her normal self-possession, and made her wonder just what his reaction was to the woman Vincenzo had recommended to care for his daughter. It was possible too that he did not like her calling his brother by his first name, for she had noticed the same slight frown a couple of times last evening when she used it.

A curt gesture with one hand indicated that she should accompany him, but he turned not in the direction of the front door she had been making for, but another, almost directly opposite and evidently a rear entrance. A brief, indeterminate glance at the front door was all she had time for, for he was already making for the other one and presumably expecting her to follow, which she did with a resigned shrug, after a second or two.

Her much shorter steps made it necessary for her to hurry if she was to keep pace with him, and she slipped past him with a breathless murmur of thanks when he stood aside to allow her through the door first. The garden she found herself in was the one she could see from her bedroom windows, and she gave herself a moment to enjoy the first refreshing breath of cool, fragrant air.

She would like to have lingered, it was what she had intended to do, but it seemed her employer had other ideas and she saw herself with little choice but to do as he wanted at the moment. Slightly ahead of her, he strode through the scented garden with scarcely a glance for the beauty around them, and rapped out a question as they rounded a huge weeping rose that trailed its heavy blossoms on the stone path.

'How long have you known my brother, Signorina Purvis?'

'I don't know.' She tried breathlessly to catch up while she considered his reason for asking. 'About four months, I suppose. He was friendly with my previous employers, and we met when I was helping out at a party one night.'

'So I understand.'

Something in his manner was puzzling her, and she frowned curiously at him from the corner of her eye, although he would hardly notice the fact. Then he stopped, so suddenly that she almost collided with him, and turned so that she found herself much too close for comfort. In the first few seconds her eyes were drawn irresistibly to the vee of dark skin at the neck of his shirt. But when she snatched her gaze from there it was to find a further distraction in the fact that the white shirt he wore was of such a thin texture that the bronzed muscular body beneath it showed through— an erotic, shadowy darkness that was infinitely disturbing in the circumstances.

'Just how—intimately do you know my brother, Signorina Purvis?'

The question was unexpected and Helen suspected its motive so that she flushed hotly. There was absolutely no reason why she should blush so readily, and because she knew it was bound to give him the wrong impression, it added to her discomfiture. Nevertheless she struggled to keep her composure, outwardly at least.

'I wouldn't call it intimate at all, *signore*,' she told him, and was thankful that she remembered the correct title to call him. But her assumption of cool confidence

seemed not to impress him and he looked down at her
with raised brows.

'So?'

It was the second time in the space of a few minutes
that he had used that faintly derisive expression, and
Helen felt herself growing resentful as well as curious.
'So!' she echoed firmly, and thought she had surprised
him. Even this early in the day the sun was strong
enough to make her screw up her eyes against it, and
she used the fact that she had come without dark glasses
as a reason for bringing this very uncomfortable conversation to an end. 'If you'll excuse me, *signore*,' she
said, 'I have to go back for my sunglasses!'

But if she had thought to get away with it, she was
soon disillusioned. A firm hand clamped over her bare
arm when she went to turn away and brought her to an
immediate halt, with hard fingers pressing into her too
responsive flesh. The black eyes had a glitter of determination that suggested to Helen he was not in the
habit of being dismissed by anyone, and he did not relax his grip even when she frowned up at him warn-
ingly.

'I should like first to hear something about you,
signorina,' he said firmly. 'I took you on trust, and it
begins to appear I might have been a little too trusting.
If that is so, *signorina*, I warn you I will have no hesitation in dismissing you at once. Isabella needs someone
more responsible than a woman who comes here simply
for her own emotional reasons. I am not paying for the
services of a starry-eyed lover, but——'

'How dare you!' Helen's eyes blazed with anger and
there was a flush in her cheeks as she faced him. Small
shadows made by the overhead trees danced in the soft
hollows of face and throat and gave a curiously ethereal
quality to her anger that smoothed out its harshness.
'I'm a fully qualified teacher, Signor Alessio, and you
don't have to take my word or Vincenzo's for that! All

it needs is a letter or a telephone call!'

Maybe he recognised the possibility of his being wrong, but if she wanted an apology she was disappointed. Nor did the steadiness of his gaze waver as he watched anger enliven her features and bring a vibrant trembling to the gentle contours of her body. Helen was seldom aroused to any kind of violent reaction, but this man had succeeded in doing it with no more than a few quietly spoken words.

'I am not questioning your qualifications, *signorina*,' he informed her coolly. 'What I question is your reason for accompanying my brother Vincenzo to Italy. I admit that I was at fault for not interviewing you myself for the post, but for once I felt myself safe in trusting my brother's word. Had I seen you first I could have made a more accurate assessment of the situation.'

'Of *what* situation?' Helen demanded. She felt suddenly as if she was getting out of her depth and there was something quite relentless about the man who towered over her and looked like nothing so much as an avenging judge. 'I agree it would have been more satisfactory if you'd interviewed me yourself; from your point of view *and* mine. In fact I was rather surprised to find any parent entrusting the care of his daughter to a stranger, sight unseen, but I supposed there were reasons for it. Maybe you were thinking of the expense of a trip to Italy simply so that you could ask me a few questions that Vincenzo could just as easily ask.' She looked up at him with bright angry eyes. 'I told myself there were a hundred reasons why you trusted Vincenzo's judgment, but apparently you've decided he was remiss in some way.'

It was a long speech, and she felt alarmingly breathless when she finished, but he had made her more angry than she ever remembered being in her life before. He was not, however, disturbed by her anger, or so it appeared, for his voice was cool and controlled, although possibly a little more harsh than usual.

'I was deceived by reticence,' he remarked after a second or two. 'It is not Vincenzo's way to say so little about a woman he has met and taken a fancy to, and I therefore accepted his word that he had found me a quiet and very respectable young woman in need of employment. Someone very capable with children and entirely suitable for my needs.'

Helen's bright hazel eyes challenged him to fault the description when applied to herself. 'I am both quiet and respectable,' she insisted firmly, 'and I was coming to the end of my term of employment when Vincenzo recommended me. I am also competent to teach and care for a young girl, so I fail to see that you have cause for complaint. Signor Alessio!'

He regarded her steadily until Helen felt suddenly less confident, seeing something in his eyes that told her there was something she had not taken into account. 'What he did not tell me was that you are also very lovely, *signorina*, and that would have given me some idea of the true situation. You are not the plain and severe woman that Vincenzo's letters led me to expect, and it is his deliberate reticence on that point that makes me suspect what I do. Vincenzo is obviously very attracted to you, he might even have declared himself in love with you, it is quite possible he has. What is of interest to me, however, is how you intend to react. The fact that you are—as you are, and not a plain, meek woman puts a very different complexion on the whole matter, as you must surely appreciate, *signorina*.'

Helen was feeling slightly lightheaded. Her cheeks were flushed and it was due in part, she suspected, to that unexpected compliment about her looks, however backhanded it might have been. What emerged quite clearly was that he did not like the possibility of Vincenzo falling in love with her, and she fiercely resented his reason for that.

'Does it offend your sense of rightness, Signor Alessio?' she enquired, finding it hard to keep her voice steady. 'The thought of Vincenzo stooping so low as to fall in love with your daughter's tutor?'

She had struck home, she saw it from the glittering blackness of his eyes, but he had such self-control, this man. Anger blazed in him, and yet his voice was as quietly controlled as ever when he answered the charge, though it was edged with steel and sent small fluttering chills down the length of her spine.

'My brother's choice of a paramour does not concern me, *signorina*,' he said, 'except when Isabella is at risk. He may fall in and out of love with the regularity of a clock ticking, and you may accept the—transient nature of your affair with him, but I will not have Isabella made a pawn in your game. If I once suspect that you are not doing your work to the very best of your ability, I shall not hesitate to get rid of you! Isabella will not come second to your affair with Vincenzo!'

Helen's hands were rolled tightly and she tried hard to control the trembling unsteadiness of her legs as she looked up at him, her eyes blazing angrily. Never in her life had she been spoken to as Guido Alessio had just spoken to her, and she had no intention of letting him get away with it.

'If that's your opinion of me, *signore*,' she told him in a throatily husky voice, 'perhaps you'd like me to leave right away! Not,' she added quickly, 'because there's a breath of truth in your assessment of my character, but because I'm not in the habit of being treated like a—a nymphomaniac! I don't expect an apology, because I don't think you're a man who ever apologises, however outrageously you behave! Will you tell Isabella, or shall I? Or shall we leave it to Vincenzo?' she added with unmistakable venom, 'since you seem to think he's good at lying!'

She turned swiftly and took the narrow stone path

back to the villa, walking on legs that felt as if they
were about to give way under her, and she listened in
vain for some sound from behind her. The only thing
she heard as she rounded the wide border of roses, however, was the firm tread of booted feet going in the
opposite direction, and for some inexplicable reason
she felt very sorry suddenly.

It was Isabella who took up the cause of whether or not
Helen should go, and she did so with a determination
that was surprising in such a dainty and doll-like creature. Isabella, as Helen had noted when she first arrived, was a charmer but used to having her way, and
with the impulsive illogicality of children, she had
decided that Helen was someone she liked and wanted
with her. The prospect of her leaving again almost before they had got to know one another did not suit at
all and she was resolved to do something about it.

'I shall hate it if you go away so soon,' she told Helen
after lunch that same day. Apparently her father had
told her the news at lunchtime, and Helen wondered
what reason he had given Isabella for the rapid de-
parture of her new tutor. 'Please, Signorina Purvis, will
you not forgive Papà and stay with me?'

Leaving her own chair, she came and sat on the arm
of Helen's. They had spent the morning in the schoolroom, but this was a rest period and they had canvas
chairs set outside the french windows of the schoolroom, enjoying the cool and the peace of the garden.
For her part, Helen would probably have been prepared to climb down, but she did not see Guido Alessio
as the kind of man to allow second chances. Nor was
she sure it would be a good idea, if she was to be regarded with suspicion for the rest of her stay.

'I don't think it's just a case of *me* forgiving your
father,' she pointed out, and put an arm around Isabella's tiny waist while she met her huge and undeni-

ably anxious dark eyes. 'It isn't as straightforward as that, Isabella. Best leave things as they are, and let your *papà* find you another tutor.'

'But I do not *want* another tutor,' Isabella insisted, and thrust out her bottom lip determinedly. 'I have told Papà that if I cannot have you to teach me, *signorina*, I will have no one at all and become the most ignorant girl in Italy!'

Helen stroked the long silky hair and shook her head. She was an endearing child, despite her strong will and her insistence on having things her way, and it was very flattering to think that she had taken to her so quickly. Isabella's light brown hair was tied back from her face, and even in the shadows the freckles showed on her fair skin, making Helen think of her yet again as much more English-looking than Italian. She could get very fond of Guido Alessio's daughter, she thought.

'I shouldn't do that,' she advised gently. 'You wouldn't punish anyone but yourself, Isabella, and I'd feel very badly about it if you really did grow into the most ignorant girl in Italy.'

'Then stay with me, yes?' Her huge eyes appealed irresistibly, and Helen could feel herself weakening; only there was more than her own consent needed to reverse the decision, and she did not believe she had the nerve to approach Guido Alessio with a plea to overlook her outburst that morning. 'Please, Signorina Purvis.' The glance was more oblique now and the dark eyes disturbingly adult in their expression. 'Tio Vincenzo will be very unhappy if you go away again.'

Mentioning Vincenzo came too close to the cause of the rift, and Helen shook her head. 'I'm here—I was here for your benefit, not your uncle's,' she pointed out, and chose to ignore Isabella's slight but expressive shrug.

'I shall speak with Papà,' she decided with an air of determination that reminded Helen of her father. She got up from the arm of Helen's chair and brushed down her dress carefully, tossing back the escaping wisps of hair from her neck. 'I shall go now before he goes back to the horses.'

'No, Isabella, I'd much rather you didn't.'

Her plea was ignored. 'I shall tell him,' Isabella said firmly, 'that you are afraid to ask if you may stay, but that you forgive him and you will stay if he agrees.'

The thought struck Helen that perhaps he would think she had put the idea into the child's head, and she saw that as the worst humiliation yet. Placing an anxious hand on Isabella's arm, she tried to restrain her. 'Please, Isabella, you don't understand the circumstances. I don't want you to say anything to your father about it; much better to let things take their course and forget about it.'

'I want you to stay!'

Isabella was insistent, childlishly stubborn and unyielding, and Helen was half out of her chair when she realised they were no longer alone. Guido Alessio had already overheard at least the last exchange, for he had come into the schoolroom unheard by either of them. For a moment only, Helen stayed as she was, half risen and with her hands on the arms of her chair, then she pulled herself upright and stood beside Isabella rather uneasily, while he crossed the room to them.

She could not imagine why he was there, unless it was to assure himself of his daughter's safety in the company of such an undesirable influence as he obviously considered her. He had been noticeably quiet during lunch and Helen had caught a swift and very meaningful glance passing between Vincenzo and his aunt, which suggested that neither of them knew of the change in circumstances as yet.

'Papà!' Isabella might have declared herself angry with her father, but she immediately took his hand and looked up at him with the warmth of love in her huge dark eyes, pressing close to his side. 'Papà, you will not let Signorina Purvis go away, will you?' she pleaded, as if the matter had not already been settled as far as the adult participants were concerned. 'Ask her to stay, Papà. *Per piacere*, Papà, *essa è simpaticissima*.'

Helen was shaking her head, so sure he would suspect her hand in the child's earnest pleas, but he said nothing for a moment, only held his daughter's small hand in his and looked steadily at Helen until she dropped her gaze. 'It seems you have a very persuasive advocate, *signorina*,' he said eventually, then addressed himself to his daughter, also in English. 'The choice was Signorina Purvis's, *piccola*, I have no wish to keep her here against her will.' He looked back to Helen again and it was impossible to tell what was going on behind those deep black eyes. 'The choice is still the *signorina*'s.'

Helen could scarcely believe that she was being given a second chance, it was the very last thing she had expected from him, but not for anything would she have let him see how much pleasure it gave her to be able to change her mind. It was a moment or two before it occurred to her that accepting the proffered olive branch would almost inevitably involve apologising for her outspokenness earlier, and that was not so acceptable.

'I think perhaps I was—I may have been a bit—hasty.' She chose her words carefully, and wished he did not watch her with such dark intensity that it made her self-conscious. 'You spoke without thinking, Signor Alessio, and so did I. For my part, I'm sorry, but I had grounds for being angry and—well, maybe you had grounds for your opinion too.'

It was difficult to tell exactly what effect her words had in the first instance, but Guido Alessio moved not a muscle, only the black eyes remained steady and unwavering, infinitely disturbing. Close to there was a magnetism about the man that affected her no matter how hard she tried to deny it. She found him fascinating to a degree that disturbed her intensely, and wished she could do something about it.

'I had not anticipated such—passion in the cause of your morals, *signorina*. As you remark, I have grounds for my opinion of your coming so willingly to Italy with Vincenzo. I cannot change that opinion, but if you wish to accept that I have the right to dismiss you should your affair with my brother affect Isabella in any way, then please change your mind about leaving. I shall not oppose the idea, except in the circumstances I have mentioned.'

So he did not intend to apologise after all. For a moment Helen felt the rise of resentment and anger, and she was almost ready to change her decision yet again. She might even have done so in the heat of the moment, but for two pairs of dark eyes watching her with such similar expressions that she caught her breath.

'Then I'll stay,' she decided in sudden breathless decision, and it was hardly believable that just for a brief moment she had seen a glint of relief in his eyes.

'So!'

To Isabella the victory was probably as sweet because she had yet again got her own way as because Helen was staying after all, but she was a warmly impulsive child and she turned swiftly and hugged Helen in her childishly thin arms. Helen herself felt strangely like laughing and crying at the same time; never in her life had she experienced so much emotional upheaval as she had since her arrival yesterday, and she wondered if she had done the right thing in climbing down after all.

Briefly, when he leaned across to smooth his daughter's hair, his hand came into contact with Helen's bare arm and she felt her pulses leap wildly in response to his touch, drawing back instinctively. He looked at her steadily, closer now and with a curious look in his eyes. 'I beg your pardon, *signorina*,' he said softly.

Helen said nothing, but strove to steady her heartbeat as it thudded hard against her ribs. There was so much more than Guido Alessio's arrogance she was going to have to cope with if she stayed on at the Villa Alessio, and she wondered if she had not perhaps bitten off more than she could chew.

Both Vincenzo and Pietro helped to run a family wine-producing business, so Helen understood, although she gathered from the amount of time they seemed to have free that they did so mostly in a supervisory capacity. Regardless of the numerous invitations issued by Vincenzo during the four days she had been there, however, Helen had stuck firmly to the schoolroom with Isabella, giving her pupil's father no reason whatever to call her to account.

The schoolroom was like nothing Helen had ever encountered before, and everything had been arranged to make learning as pleasant as possible. The room had originally been a small salon situated at the rear of the villa, and had access via the french window to the same garden she saw from her bedroom. It was nothing like the traditional classroom and at first Helen had found it quite hard to concentrate instead of looking out at the garden.

Perhaps with the idea of lessening the distraction, Isabella's desk was placed much further inside the room and away from the window, while still getting plenty of light from it. She was a good scholar and well up to the standard for her age, but several times Helen had thought of how much less isolated she would feel if she went to a school with other children of her age.

It was getting near to lunch time and for once Isabella was not bent industriously over her books, but gazing across and out of the window. The moment Helen looked up from what she was doing she caught her eye and smiled, her own dark eyes beaming with irresistible warmth. 'Will you like it here with me, *signorina*?' she asked, not for the first time, and as she always did, Helen answered unhesitatingly.

'I love it,' she said. 'I've never been anywhere half so —so near perfect.'

The reply obviously pleased Isabella, for she was smiling. 'Better than England?'

This was a new query and Helen took a second to answer it. 'Different,' she decided at last. 'It isn't possible to compare, Isabella, the two countries aren't the same. At least not the part where I come from.'

'Where do you come from, *signorina*? What place?'

Helen was aware of being led gently but surely into the path of conversation instead of learning, but she yielded with the thought that it was instruction too, in a way, if Isabella learned about another country while they talked. Her pupil had already taken her decision and sat with her book closed and her elbows propped on the desk in front of her, supporting her chin on her hands.

Helen told her about London where she had worked before coming to Italy, and about the Surrey countryside where she had been born and brought up and where her family still lived. Isabella listened with flattering attention to everything she was told, and when it was finished Helen noticed she looked wide-eyed and vaguely dreamy out of the window at the sunny garden, and there was a curious sadness about her small doll-like face.

'Have you ever been to England, Isabella?' Helen asked gently. 'You speak such good English it seems a pity not to have the chance to practise it on the natives.'

Isabella switched her gaze, but her eyes were half concealed by long thick lashes, and she was making unseen patterns on the cover of her exercise book with the tip of one finger. 'I have asked Papà to take me with him sometimes when he is there for the *saltorio*, but he never will, nor Tio Vincenzo either. I would like very much to go, but I think I must wait until I am grown up and do not need to ask permission.'

It seemed a little hard to Helen that the girl never accompanied her father on his travels, but it was not her place to say as much, so she merely smiled encouragingly and pacified her as well as she could. 'Oh, I expect there's good reason,' she told Isabella. 'You're very young, and business trips aren't really much fun, you know; no place for little girls.'

Isabella's large eyes reproached her for her thoughtlessness. 'I am ten years old, *signorina*, old enough not to be a nuisance, and I know I would enjoy seeing England.'

'I'm sure you would,' Helen agreed. 'It's very pretty for the most part and there's a lot to see if you have the time and aren't just there for business reasons.'

Isabella's expression was guileless, her dark eyes as innocent as a babe's. 'You will be going home for a holiday one day, will you not?' she asked, and quite unthinkingly Helen agreed.

'Certainly I will,' she said. 'Though not just yet, of course.'

'And would you take me with you when you go?' Helen stared for a moment realising the trap she had walked into, while Isabella pressed on with her cause. 'I would not be a trouble to you, *signorina*, and I am sure that if you asked him, Papà would agree.'

It was going to be much more difficult extricating herself from this tricky situation than she feared, Helen could see, and she felt rather mean for disappointing the child when she was faced with those appealing eyes. 'I don't think that would work, Isabella,' she told her gently. 'If your father and uncle haven't taken you with them, then I'm sure there must be a good reason for it.'

Chin propped on her clasped hands, Isabella looked across at her in silence for a moment. There was an oblique and curiously adult knowingness in her eyes that made Helen uneasy so that she hastily opened the book in front of her and flipped unseeingly through the pages. 'I think we'll go back to studying the reader, shall we?' she suggested, and bent her own head studiously over the open book.

But as Guido had warned her, Isabella was an Alessio and accustomed to having her way. She opened her book as she was told, but it remained unheeded while she watched Helen's bowed head thoughtfully. 'You are much more pretty than Signora Billings,' she observed. 'Tio Vincenzo did not like her, but he likes you, Signorina Purvis.'

Helen looked up, meaning to be firm and perhaps even scold her for speaking as she did, but it was terribly hard to be cross with a child who looked so divinely angelic and pathetic at the same time. 'Isabella, it just isn't possible,' she told her gently. 'I don't know why you're so anxious to go to England now—so quickly. You have plenty of time to travel when you're older.'

Her bottom lip pursed in reproach, Isabella bent her head over her book, but it was doubtful if she saw the words in front of her. 'I think my mother was English,' she said after several seconds, and there was nothing Helen could do to stop herself looking up so quickly and with such obvious interest. It was all the encouragement Isabella needed. 'I do not really know,' she confessed, 'because no one ever mentions her, but I believe that is why I am to speak English as well as I speak Italian. Because of my mother.'

What kind of a father was it, Helen wondered, who denied his child even the most elementary knowledge of her own mother? Surely Isabella should know what her nationality was at least, whatever had happened to part them. Maybe the compassion she felt for the child showed in her expression, for Isabella made no more pretence of bothering with her reader, but sat leaning on her elbows and gazing across at her.

'I do wonder what she was like,' Isabella confessed. 'I believe she was pretty, because Papà likes beautiful ladies.' Helen made no comment and the fact probably disappointed her informant. 'Do you not believe that?' she demanded, and Helen glanced up at her again.

'It's not something I can comment on,' she told her. 'And I don't think——'

'It is true,' her pupil insisted, her dark eyes watchful. 'Papà meets many beautiful ladies when he is travelling, and he—he *likes* them.' It wasn't hard for Helen to substitute a very much stronger word for like, for Guido Alessio was the most virile and sensual man she had ever known, but again she declined to comment. 'I just wish,' Isabella went on with stunning frankness, 'that he would marry one of the ladies he meets and bring her home to be my mother.'

For once those huge dark eyes showed just how solitary Isabella's life was, and Helen's heart went out to her, though there was nothing she could do to remedy the situation. What she could do was offer another kind of comfort, and she did so unhesitatingly and quite truthfully. 'I'm sure your own mother must have been very beautiful,' she said, 'otherwise how would she have had such a pretty daughter?'

The flattery worked, and there was already the look of a coquette in those beautiful eyes when they looked across, while one hand brushed the long brown hair back with a childishly thin hand from her neck. Smiling, she tilted her head and laughed. 'Tio Vincenzo says I am beautiful as an angel,' she told Helen, obviously delighted with the compliment. 'But I would like to be golden-haired like you, *signorina*. I shall perhaps *make* my hair golden when I am older.'

Touched by her candour and her childish conceit, Helen shook her head. 'At the moment it's more important what goes into your head than what colour it is,' she told her, deciding the subject had gone far enough. 'So let's get back to our reader, shall we?'

Isabella regarded her obliquely for a moment, mischief and speculation in her eyes. Then she laughed and tossed back her hair. '*Benissimo, signorina,*' she agreed in one of her rare lapses into Italian.

It had always been Helen's practice to sleep with her bedroom window partly open and the curtains drawn back, and she had even more reason to continue the practice in her present situation. In a room that overlooked the warm fertility of the Tuscan hills as well as the gardens at the back of the villa, it was wonderful to breathe the different scents and hear the whispering rustle of the trees while she drifted off to sleep. She had not stirred through any of the nights she had been there so far, and it was more than a week now.

It was because she was so accustomed to sleeping heavily that she woke so slowly in the early hours of one morning. Dragged muzzy-headed from her slumber, she lay quite still for a few moments, frowning into the semi-darkness and trying to decide what had disturbed her. She still rested on her right side and without moving her head she could make out the various features of the room.

The deep, dark folds of the window curtains and the huge bulk of the wardrobe were to one side of the window. The dressing-table was on the other and facing her as she lay at the moment, with the short, round-topped stool before it standing toe to toe with its own elongated shadow on the carpet. The long dressing-table mirror gleamed like grey water in the shadowy light and reflected the far side of the room as well as the foot of the bed.

It was in the mirror that she caught a reflected glimpse of movement suddenly, just beyond the railless foot of the bed, and immediately her eyes shed their sleepy droop and opened wide, while breath hissed sharply between her teeth. The urgent thudding of her heart seemed to shake the big bed and she could not move a muscle, her whole body taut and arched, fingers stiff as she watched the form of a woman materialise with startling clarity suddenly.

A long beam of bright moonlight shone in through the tall window and it was into its radiance that the figure stepped, as into a spotlight on stage. But even there, features were indistinguishable, no more than an impression. Deep shadows for eyes and mouth and cloudy dark hair surrounding a pale oval of face, and below that, what seemed to be bare shoulders shimmering whitely and almost translucent.

For the rest Helen saw only a tall, white-gowned shape that merged, unformed and indeterminate, into the darker shadows nearer the floor, so that whatever it was appeared to hover several inches above the floor. There was no movement, only a sense of watchfulness and a feeling of anticipation that became gradually unbearable.

It was during those few heart-stopping seconds, while she tried to will her paralysed body into some kind of action, that Helen's eyes were drawn like a magnet to something that gleamed and shimmered about the vision's pale column of throat. It appeared to Helen like a circlet of raindrops, and the simile did not strike her as unduly fanciful in the present circumstances. It caught the radiance of moonlight and reflected it, darting spears of light into the darkness, and shot through with rainbow colours that were too quickly gone to identify.

Helen moved at last. Her limbs shaking but obeying

her will jerkily, she scrabbled quickly round, tangling with the light covers and losing sight of the apparition for a moment or two while she extricated herself. Sitting upright, she looked at the place where it had been and saw nothing, and she gazed at the same spot for several seconds wide-eyed and trembling like a leaf.

It was gone. Whatever it had been had gone and there were only the wide beams of moonlight zooming across the bedroom carpet, and the shadowy forms of familiar objects. No sound either, but the faint sigh of the hill wind whispering through the trees. No sound, that was, until a faint and barely distinguishable click, and immediately Helen's gaze darted across to the door.

She stared at it a full ten seconds before she moved, then she turned swiftly and flicked on the bedside lamp. At once the shimmering coldness of moonlight was pushed back from the immediate vicinity of the bed by the more reassuring warmth of colour, but Helen still sat holding the bedclothes close to her chin and trembling uncontrollably.

Her heart was beating so hard that she could scarcely breathe for its clamour and it deafened her momentarily to any other sound. It was only when the stifling sense of panic lessened gradually that she became aware of other things. Of movement outside her door on the gallery, footsteps, barely audible on the muffling thickness of carpet but enough to set panic racing through her again.

She put a hand to brush beads of moisture from her brow and realised that her whole body was damp with fear, but nevertheless she tried to will herself to get out of bed. Whisperings and shufflings and the deep urgent throb of a man's voice delayed her, and then it was quiet again. Courage came after several moments of quiet, and she slid from her bed, shivering as her feet touched the sensual softness of a fur rug, reaching for the light robe that was thrown across the foot of the bed.

Without bothering to fasten it, she clutched the robe to her throat and walked soft-footed across the room, but it was a moment before she opened the door. Peering through the narrow crack she allowed herself, she saw nothing untoward. The low light that always burned on the gallery gave a comforting glow, reflected on the pale walls opposite, and the scent of carnations from a vase of them just beside her door tingled pleasantly in her nostrils, exaggerated by her hyper-active senses.

Then she took courage and opened the door wider, walking out on to the gallery and glancing in quick darting movements right and left along the narrow length of it. The door snicked to as she moved softly on bare feet, and it was a second or two before she connected the sudden appearance of Guido at the far end of the gallery with the man's voice she had heard earlier.

She knew the location of everyone's room and as far as she knew those at the far end from the stairs were unoccupied, yet Guido was leaving the one furthest away and doing so with studied quietness. It did not occur to her that if he saw her there he would want an explanation, and by the time she realised it, it was too late. When he moved away from the door he saw her.

Already he was frowning, and she anticipated his response to finding her there, outside her room and apparently wandering around the gallery in the early hours of the morning. It was as if she had become rooted to the spot, for she made no move while he came quickly towards her, but simply stayed there with one hand clutching the robe close under her chin, her heart thudding hard under his black-eyed scrutiny.

His slippered feet made little sound on the carpet,

only that slight shushing sound she had heard earlier, and she watched him, fascinated by the cat-like menace of his walk and the ranginess of his lean body wrapped around with a silk robe that she dared guess was his only covering. The response from her impetuous emotions was something she had come to expect, but she fought hard to control them as he came nearer, and her shadowed hazel eyes had a wary look when she saw the firm set of his mouth.

Whether or not she would have spoken, he did not pause to find out, but put a warning hand before his mouth and frowned, glancing back over his shoulder at Isabella's room next to hers. 'Signor Alessio——' she began, but he cut her short, speaking in a harsh whisper and drawing her beyond her own door to further along the gallery, where there was an empty room.

'Why are you not in your own room, *signorina*?' he demanded, and it was a second or two before Helen realised the significance of his words. It was a brief and barely discernible glance he gave in the direction of Vincenzo's room that gave her the clue, and she tugged to free her arm from a grip that was bruising in its strength, when she noticed it. 'Why are you wandering about out here instead of in your own bed?'

'I've *been* in my own bed!' she declared, as loudly as she dared. She was not particularly anxious to be found by anyone else, standing out here with Guido, dressed as they both were. 'Whatever ideas you have, you can take my word for it that you're wrong, Signor Alessio!'

'Then why?' he asked, and his apparent willingness to accept her word that she had not been with Vincenzo took her by surprise for a moment, making it more difficult to tell him the truth.

'I——' Her hands signalled a vague message, but somehow she felt sure he would not believe it as easily as he had her last statement. 'I thought I saw something

—someone. I don't know what it was really, I was asleep——'

'As you should be at this moment!' came the swift retort, and black eyes regarded her narrowly, sleepless and glitteringly alert. An advantage he had over Helen who, although fully aware of what was going on, still retained the dazedness of sleep in her brain.

'Something woke me up,' she went on. 'I thought— I'm sure someone was in my room. Not Vincenzo,' she added swiftly when she caught a sideways glance. 'It was a woman—I *think* it was a woman.' In her mind the shadowy figure that had assumed such terrifying clarity was growing less distinct every minute, and she shook her head in confusion. 'It looked like a woman in a white dress—a long white dress, and wearing a——' She stopped there and shook her head. Even if he believed the rest of her story, he was not going to accept the circlet of raindrops she had seen encircling the throat of her ethereal visitor.

The black eyes seemed not to have wavered, and yet to Helen's confused thinking, it appeared he was being evasive suddenly. 'A bad dream,' he suggested, in a tone that he might have used to console Isabella in a similar situation. 'It was no more than a bad dream, *no*?'

But Helen was not a little girl, and she disliked the paternal air. Rumpled from sleep and with a strange stirring of exhilaration giving brightness to her eyes, she looked up at him and found his gaze resting on her mouth, soft and uncertain, the lips slightly parted. 'Please don't talk to me as if I was Isabella,' she told him in a low whisper. 'I saw *some*thing as clearly as I see you now, and it frightened me.'

'Ah!' Apparently he understood that, and the pressure of his fingers about her arm was much less bruisingly hard now, the tips of them light and soothing, almost seductive as he turned her back towards her room. When he moved beside her, his body beneath the silk robe touched her lightly at every step, and she found the contact infinitely disturbing, so that for a second or two she was in no mind to argue with his theory. 'I wish I could convince you that you have nothing to be afraid of,' he said close to her ear, as he bent to open her bedroom door, but the soft click it made when it opened reminded her, and she turned and looked up at him.

'I heard the door close,' she whispered, stopping in the doorway. 'I heard it quite plainly just before I switched on the light, and I was awake and sitting up then. I couldn't have dreamed that. I heard footsteps too,' she recalled, 'and—and voices, especially a man's voice.' She looked up at him earnestly, her hazel eyes bright and anxious between their drooping lashes. '*Your* voice?'

He neither confirmed nor denied it, but watched her again with that same disturbing intensity until she could no longer still the fluttering urgency of her pulse. 'If you are fearful that someone is in your room, I will reassure you,' he said in the same deep soft voice that was barely more than a whisper. Drawing level with her in the doorway, he raised a questioning brow. '*Posso?*'

Her brief nod gave the permission he asked, and he went past her into her bedroom, looking around briefly before returning to switch on the brighter overhead lights. The room was, of course, empty save for the two of them, and yet Helen felt it had a curiously pregnant air that made small cold sensations slide one after another down the length of her back.

'You see?' Her gaze fixed on his broad back, Helen hastily switched it to the floor at her feet when he turned and came back across the room to her. 'There is nothing here to give you cause for alarm, do you agree?'

She nodded, then caught her breath when he leaned forward to switch off the overhead light, bringing a brief and unexpected contact again as he did so. 'Yes, of course,' she whispered breathlessly. 'I'm sorry I bothered you.'

'Now will you try to go back to sleep?'

Again she nodded, trying not to resent the fact that he still sounded much too paternal when he comforted her. He was so close that she had only to breathe a little more deeply for that alarmingly disturbing contact to happen again, and it seemed there was little she could do to prevent it. She was not consciously aware of wanting to keep him there, and yet the need clamoured against her common sense and almost overpowered it.

Her voice was soft and breathlessly husky and the words oddly slurred, as if she was already on the brink of sleep again, even though she had never felt more alive. 'There *was* someone,' she whispered, 'but as long as whoever it was doesn't come back——'

'You have my word on it!'

She looked up then and met the black eyes directly, lost for a moment in the gleaming depths of them. 'Then I must accept your word for it,' she said. 'Thank you, *signore*.'

She would have looked away, but somehow her gaze seemed to be held so fast by those black eyes that she could do nothing but look into them. She shivered when he rested his hands lightly on her waist and drew her towards him until the touch of his body fired her senses and filled her with an indescribable need. He slid his hands round behind her and pressed them, flat-palmed, in the small of her back, and all the time his eyes never left hers. glitteringly dark between thick short lashes.

Through the silk robe his hard masculinity taunted her own more hesitant reaction, and each breath touched her with the long vee of bronzed flesh that reached almost as far as his waist, warming her soft skin where her own robe had fallen open. She should have moved away, Helen knew it, and put an end to what was a dangerously provocative situation, but somehow she was unable to move a muscle except in response to the hands that pressed her ever closer.

Tipping back her head, her long lashes lay on flushed cheeks as he bent his head, and the black eyes were hidden except for a shadowed slit of gleaming darkness that brought shivers of anticipation to her whole body. His mouth was no longer stern, but half-smiling in a way that thrust out the sensual lower lip temptingly, brushing her warm mouth lightly until her lips parted.

Long hard fingers pressed into her back, sliding slowly forward and up under her arms, coaxing and persuasive as she reached up to put her arms about his neck. Her eyes were closed, her lips trembling with anticipation of the promised kiss, but the promise was never fulfilled, for in that moment they both heard the same irresistible cry.

It was the faint, unmistakable cry of a child, quivering and uncertain and bordering on tears, and it snatched away the magic of the moment in a second. Guido lifted his head, looking down at her with the lingering heat of passion in his eyes, but the spontaneous abandon that had possessed them both for those few moments was gone, and he was once more the man in control.

He drew back, holding her at arms' length and looking down at her flushed face and downcast eyes. 'I have to apologise,' he said, and Helen looked up dazedly, almost unbelieving. Drawing the robe more closely around him, he shook his head. 'I made certain remarks about you and Vincenzo earlier——'

'Please don't!'

She had tried to stop him from apologising, but he was set on making his own situation quite clear, she guessed, and he went on, his words sounding too cool and easy for Helen's spinning head to accept. 'In the circumstances I am doubly sorry that this happened, and I hope you will accept my word that nothing like it will occur again.'

'Of course!' Her voice sounded oddly harsh and unsteady, and Helen could not understand why she resented his apology so much.

He still stood watching her, as if something in her manner disturbed him. 'You will be O.K.? You are no longer afraid?'

What would he do, Helen wondered, if she told him she was afraid to stay alone? Quickly dismissing the very idea of it, she shook her head. 'I'll be fine,' she told him, then lifted her head quickly when Isabella called again from the next room.

'I will go,' he said, still in the same soft half-whisper that stroked along her back like a fingertip touch. 'Go back to bed, *signorina*, and try to sleep.'

She nodded without speaking and he lingered a second longer, until Isabella's plaintive voice called again. Turning abruptly, he left her, closing the door carefully behind him, and Helen stood for a moment in the middle of the room with her hands clasped together tightly, and sleep had never been further from her brain.

She was in the act of turning back to her bed when she heard him speak to someone out on the gallery. Not Isabella, it was a woman's voice and she thought she recognised it, wondering what Signorina Alessio would have to say about her eldest nephew leaving his daughter's governess's room in the early hours of the morning.

CHAPTER THREE

For several days following Guido's nocturnal visit to her bedroom Helen lived on tenterhooks, waiting to hear something about it from Signorina Alessio, for she was firmly convinced it was his aunt she had heard speak to him just after he left her. So far, however, the older woman had made no mention of it, and that seemed somehow out of character for the woman Helen believed her to be.

It was true that Helen had been the target of several long and very meaningful looks, but no verbal reference was forthcoming, so that she began to wonder just what explanation Guido had made to account for his being with her at that hour of the night. Unless he had simply allowed his aunt to put the obvious construction on it and then forbidden her to say anything. He was, Helen felt sure, quite capable of laying down the law, even to his formidable aunt, and getting away with it.

She did not altogether understand her own reticence where Vincenzo was concerned, and it still rather surprised her that she had so far said nothing to him. The only reason she could think of for her silence was that inevitably Vincenzo would make a fuss, whether or not he had cause to. He might well laugh at the idea of her ghostly visitor, but he was less likely to find Guido's part in the incident very amusing, and she had no desire at all to cause trouble between them.

When the incident had gone unremarked for several days she began to relax and tried to put it to the back of her mind, although it proved harder to do than she expected. The recollection of being in Guido's arms for those few moments was much more clear in her mind

54

than that of the more ethereal visitation.

For the next couple of weeks she was kept pretty busy, and she saw scarcely anything of Guido, apart from at mealtimes, when she sometimes had the opportunity to study him unobserved while he talked to the others. Isabella's schooling took most of her time, and Vincenzo made sure she did not want for something to do during the evenings and at weekends. It was Vincenzo who explained about the festival of Saint Catherine, or Santa Caterina, as he called it.

Isabella had mentioned it briefly, but it was Vincenzo who put her in the picture. Santa Caterina was the small town she could see from her bedroom window, and it celebrated its saint's day each September seventeenth with processions and fireworks and a general holiday. A religious procession began the day, followed by more lighthearted entertainments in the afternoon and evening with fireworks to round off the celebrations.

'It sounds fun,' said Helen, ready and willing to join in.

'It is perhaps a little—small-town,' Vincenzo said, with the air of one who has travelled a lot, 'but it is a lot of fun, Helen, and I shall insist that you come!'

'I'd love to,' she assured him, and immediately thought of her charge who seemed to have so few excitements in her young life. 'Isabella too?'

'Everyone joins in,' Vincenzo claimed extravagantly, his brown eyes glowing darkly with anticipation. 'Why, even Guido has been known to put in an appearance occasionally. Tia Olivia will go in the morning to see the procession to the church, and then in the afternoon I go with Pietro, Bianca and Isabella. But it is the evening festivities that are the most fun.' He winked an eye and left his meaning in no doubt at all, then laughed. 'It is the time for more—adult amusements!' He slid an arm around her and brought his face down to hers, pressing his cheek against hers so that his breath warmed her skin. 'That is when you and I will have most fun, eh, my Helen?'

'I'd certainly like to go and see the fun,' Helen agreed, but she obviously did not sound as carried away by the prospect of the evening he had planned for her as Vincenzo thought she should. 'Pietro and Bianca won't mind if I join in the family outing, will they?'

'But of course not!' He pulled a rueful face. 'I very much doubt if poor Bianca will be going this year, for with the *bambino* so close it will not be safe for her in such a crowd. But Pietro will come, I expect, and also Isabella. Then you will see how we enjoy ourselves in Tuscany, eh?'

His excitement was infectious, and she laughed with him, unable to resist the prospect of anything that promised to be so full of colour and pageantry. 'I can't wait to see it all. On the seventeenth, you said?' He nodded, turning his head when Guido came in from the stable.

As usual he had been missing for most of the day, and, as he most often was during the day, he was dressed for riding—light trousers and shirt and those thick-heeled boots that gave him such a firm tread. He murmured a greeting, throwing down the cane he carried before going over to pour himself a drink without even stopping to take off his gloves first. Then he turned suddenly and looked at them, and there was a narrowness about his scrutiny that brought unbidden colour to Helen's cheeks. She had never minded Vincenzo putting his arm around her, but somehow that black-eyed look of Guido's made her very uneasy.

'You were telling Signorina Purvis about the Festa della Santa Caterina?' he asked, and Vincenzo grinned, one eyelid flickering briefly.

'I am telling her how much she will enjoy it,' he said. 'Especially the evening time!'

'So!'

The black eyes were firmly on Helen suddenly, and she hastily avoided meeting them while she wondered what particular interpretation to put on that favourite expression of his this time. If she could have shrugged off Vincenzo's encircling arm without offending his sensitive ego, she would have done, for it was so difficult for her, whenever she was near Guido, not to remember that moment in her bedroom when she had been so willing to be kissed.

'Will you be going, Signor Alessio?' she asked, and somehow managed to stop her voice from sounding as if she hoped he was going to say he would.

It often struck her as odd, too, that she could have been so intimately close to him for those few minutes and yet still address him by his formal title. But he had never done anything about it, and it was surely his place to make the change, not hers as an employee. 'Perhaps I will go,' he replied eventually. 'It is an affair in which most of us play some part, even if only as onlookers.'

'You'll be taking Isabella?'

He darted a quick glance from her to his brother and back again, then lifted his broad shoulders in a shrug, peeling off his riding gloves as he finished his drink and set the glass down. 'I doubt it, *signorina*. That is something Vincenzo enjoys, and I have no wish to deprive him of the pleasure.'

He would obviously have left it there, but Helen had the strangest feeling there was something behind his last words, although she had no idea what it might be. 'Oh, but surely she'd rather go with her father,' she suggested impulsively, and Guido eyed her for a moment in silence.

'I imagine so,' he said, and turned to go.

Watching him move away with that long, easy step, Helen frowned curiously and shook her head. When the door closed behind him, she turned to Vincenzo and heaved her shoulders resignedly. 'I don't begin to understand your brother,' she confessed, and he laughed.

Turning her into his arms, he kissed her lips lightly. 'Then do not trouble yourself to try,' he advised. 'Just tell me that you will go to the *festa* with me, and I do not care whether Guido goes or not.'

'Of course I'll come,' Helen said, but she still wondered why it mattered so much whether or not Guido would be there too, when she had Vincenzo for company.

As Vincenzo had suggested, Bianca did not go with them to the *festa*, it would have been most unwise in her present condition to have to contend with the surging mass of people, no matter how good-natured the jostling might be. Santa Caterina was so small that Helen wondered how on earth it contained all the people who came to swell the normal population to three or four times its normal size.

The weather was perfect, and the decorated floats decked in the last of the summer flowers, as well as vines and grapes from the wine harvest, looked as lushly prolific as the countryside around and the comfortably built local women with their dark-eyed *ragazzi*. It was noisy and colourful and Helen enjoyed every minute of it, standing between Pietro and Vincenzo, and holding Isabella's hand as she balanced on Vincenzo's shoulders to see better.

The air was hot and dusty and smelled of crushed flowers, of donkeys, and hot, oily food and too many people in one small town, but she would not have missed it for anything. It was getting dark when she and Vincenzo walked back to the car with Pietro, whose job it was to see Isabella safely home to bed while they continued on into the night with most of the other revellers.

Isabella was heavy-eyed and smiling in a way that showed how much she had enjoyed the change from normality, and Helen was strangely touched when she wound her thin little arms about her neck and kissed her. '*Buona notte*, Helen,' she murmured, glancing from her to Vincenzo. 'Have fun, yes?'

She had never before used the familiarity of Helen's first name, and Helen hoped she was not going to be pulled up for it, as she had no personal objection. Vincenzo, however, lifted her into his arms and kissed her soundly, holding her very close for a moment, and smiling with his dark, velvet-brown eyes. 'You are too saucy, *polla mia*,' he told her. 'You must not become too familiar without permission or your *papà* will hear of it, and then—*mamma mia*, after all he has told you about being polite? Brr-r-r!'

He shuddered very realistically, but Isabella was obviously not in the least frightened by his threat to tell her father; she laughed. 'You would not tell Papà,' she assured him confidently, and he too laughed.

They knew one another very well, these two, Helen thought, and felt a certain sadness that Guido seemed not to have the same rapport with his own child. Hugging her close, Vincenzo kissed her again, a noisy, boisterous kiss on her cheek that made her giggle. 'Brat!' he scolded laughingly. '*Buona notte, piccola,* sleep well!'

When he set her on her feet, Pietro saw her into the front of his car, and she turned to wave when they drove off a few moments later. Helen was always touched by the brothers' obvious love for their little niece, and especially Vincenzo's, for he so obviously adored her, so that she smiled up at him as they turned back towards the crowded streets and the sound of music.

Catching her eye, he bent his head and kissed her, heedless of the people around, for it was *festa*, and the time for kissing pretty girls. 'Now we will have our kind of fun, my Helen, eh?' he whispered, holding her close in the curve of his arm. 'But first some *vino*, *si*? To put us in a mellow mood, and to warm the blood.'

Helen felt her blood was warmed enough, and certainly Vincenzo seemed in no further need of intoxication, so that she merely smiled and tried to keep her feet firmly on the ground. 'I hope no one will tell Guido about Isabella calling me Helen,' she ventured, almost knocked off her feet by a couple hurrying about their own business and oblivious of anyone else. 'I don't mind in the least, Vincenzo.'

They stopped right there in the middle of the narrow pavement, so that the passing crowd were obliged to make a detour around them, and seemed not to mind in the least. His hands on her arms, Vincenzo looked down into her face, lifting her chin with one hand, then bending to kiss her mouth again—more lingeringly this time, and putting both arms around her while still in possession of her mouth, pulling her close until she placed her hands on his chest between them.

'*Carissima!*' He breathed the endearment against her lips, and his eyes had a dark brilliance that made her shiver suddenly. '*Mia carina*, Helen. *Ti amo, carissima, ti amo!*' His mouth was close to her ear, then on her neck, his lips pursed and light, then hot and forceful, and the hands that held her seemed to be trembling.

'Vincenzo!' She managed to push him a little away so that she could look up into his face and see the gleaming darkness of his skin, beaded with moisture across the broad brow and shadowed upper lip. 'Not here in the middle of Santa Caterina, please. Let's—let's walk a while and see the crowds and listen to the music.'

There was an increasing noise of brass and drums, beating incessantly in the hot dusty air, and she was not even sure if he had heard her. He reached for her again and she stepped back, apologising hastily to a stout bearded man who smiled in return and speculated with bright dark eyes. The band was nearer now, and with it a whole crowd of people dancing, skipping along in front and behind it, and alongside wherever the narrow footpath gave room.

Sleepy-eyed children gazed in wonder from the vantage of parental shoulders, and even stout *signoras* gazed at their spouses with the lure of *festa* in their eyes. The band drowned whatever Vincenzo was saying, and he frowned over his shoulder at the approaching crowd, then cried aloud when Helen was snatched bodily from his hands and swept into the swarm that followed the band.

Her own momentarily frightened face was the only one not smiling, and someone tugged at her hand, making her one of a line of young people skipping along behind the pounding brass and percussion. She could see nothing for bobbing heads and smiling faces, and there was a breathless urgency about those around her that communicated itself to her as she was hauled along, both hands held now by hot, strange hands that clamped her too close to escape.

Hemmed in as she was, she had no idea where she had left Vincenzo, or how far she had come, but she was hot and breathless and just a little frightened of the endless, driving energy of those around her. They sang and laughed, and some of them spoke to her, but always in Italian which she could not understand, and she shook her head. It was like being deaf, surrounded by noise and unable to distinguish a single word.

Then she was snatched from the melée by an arm about her waist and drawn from the hold of those imprisoning hands, as if by magic. She could think only of Vincenzo, and that he had followed and somehow got to her, but something about the hard, lean body that she leaned against while she recovered her breath was alarmingly familiar suddenly. Lifting her head sharply, she looked up with wide, startled eyes into the dark sternness of Guido's face.

'Guido!'

Her breathless murmur was barely audible, and she realised only when she had spoken that she had used his name with the same naturalness Isabella had used hers a short time ago. His right arm was around her still and held her close enough for the regular, hard beat of his heart to pulse against her like a drum. A dark jacket and slacks complemented a white shirt that opened at the neck in a deep vee, exposing the length of his throat and the first glimpse of dark hair on his chest.

The arm that held her eased a little, but did not let her go, and one hand lay snugly on her waist just below the curve of her breast. 'Where is Vincenzo?' he asked, and for a moment Helen gazed at him uncomprehendingly.

Her whole body was responding to his nearness, and she could think of nothing else. Vincenzo was almost forgotten, pushed somewhere to the hazy distance in her mind by the proximity of the man who had snatched her from the crowd and now held her in the curve of his arm as if it was not only the most natural thing in the world for him to do, but as if he had every right to do it.

Helen grappled with her spinning senses, and arrived at what she thought might be his main concern. 'Isabella's all right,' she told him. 'Pietro left for home with her only a little time ago.'

'I know.' He cut short her explanation as he so often did. 'I can trust Pietro to take care of her.' The black eyes looked down, enveloping her in their gleaming depths. 'Which is more than Vincenzo is capable of doing for you, it seems,' he added. 'How did you become parted, *signorina?*'

'Oh, must you!' Helen's cry of protest was instinctive, born of the need to be closer to him than he seemed prepared to allow with that formal title he gave her. She caught her bottom lip between her teeth when she saw the swift arch of his brows, and shook her head. 'I suppose it's your way of putting me firmly in my place after I called you by your first name,' she went on with a catch in her voice. 'I'm sorry, *signore*, but it *is* a festival, and everyone seems so—so friendly.'

In the circumstances she quite expected to have that comforting arm withdrawn, but instead it remained where it was, and the long fingers at her waist moved just slightly in a gesture that seemed to stroke her responsive flesh through the thin cotton dress she wore. 'Perhaps a little too—friendly?' he suggested. 'Is that perhaps why you are no longer in Vincenzo's company?'

Helen remembered that she had been objecting, though mildly, about Vincenzo becoming too ardent in what she considered too public a place, but she shook her head rather than let Guido think it was her reason for leaving his brother. 'Nothing like that,' she denied. 'I was caught up in a crowd following the band, and I don't know what happened to him. I was—swept along with no option but to join them, as you saw.'

He continued to look at her and she found the experience both disturbing and enjoyable, like the gentle caress of his fingers. 'Then since you appear to have lost your partner for the *festa*, perhaps you will permit me to take his place,' he suggested.

He had pulled her into the doorway of an old house. A tall, stone house whose paint was flaking and its shutters broken, faintly sinister in the fading daylight, but with a deep doorway that offered the perfect refuge. 'There doesn't seem much chance of my finding him in this,' Helen whispered huskily. 'I—I don't think it's even worth trying, is it?'

'I would say it is impossible,' Guido agreed. 'Therefore, if you will allow me, I will do my best to see that you enjoy the *festa*. Would you like a drink?'

Only now did she realise just how thirsty she was, and she smiled up at him eagerly. 'Oh yes, please, I'm thirsty!'

Walking with him through the narrow streets of Santa Caterina was much different from being with Vincenzo, and she once or twice found herself musing on the possibility of Guido ever standing in the middle of a crowded pavement to kiss a girl. Several times she dismissed the idea without finding an answer, but she could never quite suppress the desire to find out by personal experience.

He did not politely hold her arm to ensure their staying together, but held her hand instead, his strong fingers firmly enclosing hers and keeping her close to his side. She had no idea where he was taking her, nor did she care, for she felt suddenly so much more affected by the general air of abandonment. From necessity Guido shortened his normally long step, and the jostling throng of people passing both ways along the narrow street pressed in on them from all sides, but Helen smiled. Wherever Guido chose to lead, she would go.

Whether or not it was the same noisy band that was coming towards them, she couldn't tell, but the inevitable crowd of revellers accompanied it, and at one point she came close to being whisked away again. This time, however, Guido plucked her back before she disappeared, and from then on kept his arm tightly around her waist.

In the plane trees that lined the main street, coloured lights came on with the encroaching darkness, and the street cafés were filled to overflowing, so that Helen wondered if she was likely to get her drink after all. But just when she had resigned herself to being thirsty, she was whisked around a corner and into an even narrower street where both the noise and the crowd were less. It was without lights too, except for that which came from a small *taverna* part way along, where deep yellow light spilled across the pavement from open door and windows.

For the first time too, she noticed that there was a moon, huge and soft and honey-yellow, deepening the blackness of tall narrow houses with gaping doorways and flat, blank windows. 'Where are we?'

She looked up at him as she asked, and at once the black eyes were turned on her so that she shivered without warning. The hand at her waist tightened its clasp briefly, and a hint of a smile seemed to hover around that sometimes cruel mouth. 'Do you not trust me, Helen?'

His use of her first name in that deep, quiet voice brought a fluttering urgency to her pulse, even when she recalled that it was at her own request he was being less formal. 'Of course I trust you,' she assured him huskily. 'I just wondered where we were, that's all. I've never been to Santa Caterina before, this is all new to me.'

'It is a very old part of the town, away from the bright lights,' he told her. 'But there are always bars to be found in the older quarters and wine that is grown locally. You have said you are thirsty, and we should find something here that will satisfy you.'

Her thirst was indeed satisfied, but Helen felt slightly more lightheaded by the time they left the little bar and walked back along the moonlit street. It was always so difficult to tell what was going on behind those deep, dark eyes and she studied him for a moment as she walked beside him.

'Are you sure you don't have your own plans for this evening?' she asked. 'I mean, if you should be somewhere—with someone——' She stumbled over the words, but he did nothing to help, only looked at her steadily. 'I mean, I don't want to spoil your evening, and you can't have planned to spend the *festa* on your own, surely.'

'It need not concern you how I meant to spend my evening,' he told her quietly. 'I am content with the way things are.'

She ventured an upward glance. 'You didn't come this afternoon with Isabella and the rest of us.'

For a moment she thought he was not going to answer her, but eventually he did, though without looking at her. 'Vincenzo likes to bring Isabella to the *festa*,' he said, and something in his voice warned her that it was the last such question he meant to answer. 'He does so every year, just as he takes her to the Christmas Festival.'

'And you don't mind?'

Briefly he turned and looked at her, but his eyes were unfathomable as they so often were. 'It is only fair,' he said, but made no explanation of the rather oblique answer, only went on quickly before she had time to ask anything else. 'I hope you are not bored or disappointed with your evening so far, Helen?'

She recovered herself hastily. 'Oh, but of course I'm not!' she denied. 'I wasn't trying to——'

'Would you like to watch the dancing?' He cut her short, and it was clear he was making it as plain as possible that he would not discuss anything to do with his family. 'There is what I believe you call a local hop. It is perhaps not what you are accustomed to, but it can be amusing to watch, and I think you will enjoy it.'

Feeling rather snubbed, Helen glanced up at him, trying to guess if he wanted to go or not. 'I suppose you don't dance, do you?' she ventured.

'Not the kind of dancing that they do in Santa Caterina on *festa* night,' he agreed with a quirk of humour, and looked down at her as they turned again into the main street. 'I am sorry.'

It was hard to make out just what he was apologising for, but she had a vague idea that he might be sorry for virtually snubbing her a few minutes before, and she looked up at him and smiled. 'It doesn't matter,' she told him. 'It really doesn't.'

They were back in the thick of the throng once more, and there were so many distractions that by the time they had made their way to the place where the dancing was being held the event was well under way. Only by a bit of insistent pushing was Guido able to find room for them on one of the abandoned floats from the procession, and Helen settled thankfully, resting her tired feet and leaning against him for support.

The dance floor itself was a makeshift affair, consisting simply of planks laid side by side on the grass and dangerously uneven in places, while the band was either the same confusion of brass and drums they had heard in the street earlier, or one very similar. The dancers were a cross-section of any small Italian town, and endowed with the Latin ability to enjoy themselves completely without inhibition.

Obviously a good deal of *vino* had been consumed during the day, but Helen felt convinced that most of the exuberance and energy shown by those on the dance floor owed much more to sheer excitement than to drink. Older couples were attempting to keep pace with their younger compatriots to the endless and tuneless noise from the band, and some of the youngsters displayed amazing agility in their own version of the latest dances.

One girl, Helen noticed after a while, whirled and spun like a dervish, her white pleated skirt swinging almost waist-high, while her ample figure swayed erotically, much to the delight of her own partner and others. It was while she was close to the edge of the plank floor that she tripped suddenly and went sprawling, almost at their feet.

She was unhurt and the crowd's response was a loud yell of laughter, accompanied in some cases by some obviously ribald observations on her display. The girl got up, boldly uncaring, and brushed herself down, tugging the necklace she wore round to the front again, and it was that last gesture that caught Helen's eye. The jewellery was obviously fake, but it glittered brightly in the artificial light, like a circle of raindrops, shot through with rainbow tints, and it immediately struck a note.

She had been half-leaning against Guido, held in the careless circle of his arm, and she leaned forward suddenly, staring at the cheap, glittering stones as if hypnotised. The girl was gone, back into her wild routine, when Guido leaned forward too and his hand curved into Helen's waist, drawing her gaze to him instead.

She did not remember that she had told him nothing of the necklace she had seen her nocturnal visitor wearing, and her eyes were dark and puzzled as she coped with an almost vanished memory. Guido was frowning at her curiously. 'You recognise it?' he asked, without referring specifically to the girl's necklace, and Helen nodded. 'How, Helen?'

She shook her head. 'I've seen it—I think I've seen it.' She looked at him for a second then shook her head. 'Don't you remember, she was wearing it? The woman you said I'd imagined; who came into my room that night.'

'I did not know——' Again his hand squeezed hard into her waist. 'I did not hear you say anything about the Tears of Venus, I thought you had merely seen the —the figure standing there.'

The dancing was forgotten, even though the insistent pounding of the music thudded in their heads still, and after a moment or two, Guido dropped down on to the grass and reached up his arms for her. She swung clear of the float and was held for a moment at eye level, aware of the glowing darkness of his eyes as they watched her.

Then he set her on her feet and took her hand as a

matter of course, leading her away from the crowd, and to where there was only the moonlight and the twisted armies of olive trees at the edge of town behind them. Other couples had sought the quieter part of the ground, away from their noisier friends, but none walked together with such a silence between them, and Helen felt strangely lost suddenly.

It was cooler too, away from the crowd, and she shivered slightly. No comforting arm was forthcoming in this instance, however, and she put her free hand to the chilled flesh of her upper arm, hugging it across her breast, almost defensively. They climbed a steep slope that gave an almost bird's-eye view of the dance floor, and in the shadow of the encroaching olive trees Guido stopped and turned to face her.

'Tell me what you saw,' he said, quietly but with such authority that she knew he was no longer Guido, but Signor Alessio again. 'When you saw someone in your room, tell me what you saw, Helen.'

She had the strangest feeling that she was under interrogation, and she clasped her hands tightly together, feeling bereft suddenly without his support. 'I told you all I know at the time,' she reminded him. 'I woke up and saw a woman reflected in the mirror. She was tall and in a long white dress, and she had a necklace—I don't know, some kind of a necklace round her throat. It looked like—it reminded me of a circle of raindrops. I only saw it in the mirror—I only saw *her* in the mirror. When I turned round she was gone.'

'But you clearly saw the necklace? She was definitely wearing it?'

'How else could I have known about it?' she asked.

He moved closer and she was again enveloped in that dark, unfathomable gaze. 'Vincenzo could have told you about it,' he suggested. 'The Tears of Venus have always fascinated him.'

'The—Tears of Venus?'

In fact she had never really thought of that circle of raindrops as actually existing, only as part of a vague and scarcely believable dream. Seeing the same thing around the neck of that girl just now had come as a shock, and Guido had noticed it. She looked up at him and shook her head, trying to detach fact from illusion.

'It exists? The necklace I saw that night—it does exist?'

He admitted it, although Helen had the feeling he would rather not have done. 'It was made for my great-grandmother during the last century. Right here in Santa Caterina.'

She glanced down the hill to where smoky yellow light picked out the board dance floor and silhouetted dancers and watchers alike in a restless, shifting pattern of shadows. 'That girl——' she ventured.

'One of the di Sentis women. The craftsman who made the original did not destroy the design, and a cheap copy was made just after the last war for the wife of the mayor. The women of the family wear it on occasions like this to—show off.'

But Helen's mind had dispensed with the girl and her cheap imitation. She was recalling the one she had seen gleaming around the throat of the figure at the end of her bed. 'If the necklace exists,' she ventured after a moment or two, 'then so must the woman who was wearing it. Doesn't she, Guido?'

'That need not concern you!'

The harshness of the rebuff, even though she had been expecting something of the sort, startled her and she shook her head in silent protest. Standing with both hands in his pockets, he looked adamant and unyielding, and showed that hint of cruelty on his firm mouth that she hated to see, while she coped with a sense of loss she did not fully understand.

Her eyes looked enormous, and seemed to dominate her small face, her lips slightly parted as she glanced at him, trying to come to terms with a sudden change of mood. Only minutes ago she had been laughing and happy in his company, and now she felt confused and half afraid. 'I was simply trying to get you to admit her existence,' she told him in a very unsteady voice. 'You insisted it—she was something I'd dreamed up, and now——'

'Now that you are aware she was not it makes no difference!' he declared firmly. 'You have no more call to concern yourself with the matter than before!' Yet he did not let it drop completely, but regarded her with slightly narrowed eyes; still the aloof autocrat who bore no resemblance to the man she had enjoyed the past few hours with. 'Did you mention anything of that night to Vincenzo?' he asked, and Helen looked up at him unbelievingly.

'Do you think I would?' she asked.

From the way he shrugged with such carelessness it might be supposed he had forgotten all but the fact of the strange woman in her room, and Helen's hands rolled tightly into themselves as she fought for self-control. 'In view of your—friendship, it is possible,' he said quietly.

'And if I had do you suppose Vincenzo wouldn't have said something to you?' she whispered.

The black eyes were so shadowed that it was impossible for her to guess their expression, but his mouth had a grim tight look, as if he hated the implication. 'It would have been possible to mention the other matter without telling him that you had seen me also,' he told her. 'Although even Vincenzo would have difficulty making a fuss about anything as—uneventful, surely.'

Only her eyes showed the hurt she felt, and she turned from him quickly for fear he noticed it. Hands on her bare arms, she hunched her shoulders in a wary defensive gesture and spoke over her shoulder. 'I'm getting a bit chilly,' she said, her voice barely audible. 'I'd like to go home, if you wouldn't mind.'

'Helen!'

He spoke so softly that she knew he had been touched at last, and when she looked he was closer than she realised. Then suddenly, without warning, the heavens seemed to explode overhead and scatter a cascade of coloured stars across the night sky. Startled, she turned quickly, looking up at the same time and clumsy on the uneven ground.

Whether or not she would have fallen, Guido reached out for her and drew her close, folding her into his arms, her face pressed into his shoulder. His hands soothed and comforted, one curved about her shoulders, the other stroking lightly over her pale golden hair, while she clung to him with her cheek pressed to the steady thudding beat of his heart.

She did not want to move or to open her eyes, but when she did she could see the vee of dark skin at the open neck of his shirt and noticed how urgently it throbbed with a pulse at the base of his throat. It seemed to be the one vulnerable thing about an otherwise impregnable man, a weakness that fascinated her as much as his strength did, so that she slid a hand up over the broadness of his chest and touched the pulsing spot lightly with a finger-tip.

His arms tightened suddenly, making her catch her breath, and lilting, musical Italian words breathed against the softness of her neck. Raising her head, the deep black eyes filled her vision for a moment before he found her mouth, and she raised her parted lips to his, felt the flood of passion when they touched, and yielded unhesitatingly.

There was a burning urgency in the kiss and a vigorous dominance in the body that strained her to him, releasing in her an abandoned joy that sang through her veins like rich wine. Overhead the bursts of coloured fire continued, darting flashes of brilliance across her closed lids, but dimmed by the fierce possession of his mouth.

Opening her eyes slowly, she looked up into his face, and her hands stroked his broad back in a caress there was no resisting. Beneath the thin jacket, the powerful muscles responded to her touch, and again that hard searching mouth took possession, dominant and irresistible.

Somewhere nearby a voice was raised, and she was reminded hazily of the night he had come to her room, the night she had seen that mysterious figure in the moonlight, its throat encircled by something Guido called the Tears of Venus. But tonight she was not jolted back to reality by Isabella's crying, for Isabella was safely home in bed, and the promise she had seen in Guido's eyes that night was being fulfilled.

But he was drawing back, slowly, cupping her flushed face in his palms, his lips lingering on hers as if only reluctantly leaving them. When she looked at him she saw the shadowed arrogance of his features less clearly, except for his eyes, and there the enigma of mystery was already returning, as he eased her away from the supporting strength of his body.

'I made a promise,' he reminded her, as if explanation was needed. 'I had meant to keep that promise, Helen.'

'Oh, but——'

He stilled her smiling protest with his mouth, then dropped his hands to her waist. 'It is the festival of Santa Caterina,' he said, soft-voiced. 'It is the custom to kiss pretty girls—that must be my excuse.'

Her mouth still burned from his kiss and she could not believe he was apologising. She did not want him to be sorry about it, and she lifted a hand to press one fingertip to his lips, smiling a curious, sleepy kind of smile and needing the warmth of his arms again. He still held her, but lightly, his hands at her waist and preventing that thrilling contact between them.

'Guido.'

She said it softly, half whispering, but she almost gasped aloud when someone came upon them so quickly it was as if he had sprung from the ground. Breathing hard, Vincenzo stopped only about a foot away and his dark eyes had none of the velvety softness she was familiar with. Very obviously he had come up the slope from the dance-area at a speed that had taken all his breath and he stood silent for a moment, only the fury in his eyes showing what he had seen.

Guido dropped his hands from her waist, but slowly, so as not to give the impression that he did so with any sense of guilt, and he looked at his brother with his unfathomable eyes for a moment before he spoke. 'Where have you been?' he asked coolly. 'Helen was lost in the crowd and frightened. You should take more care of your partner, Vincenzo.'

Whatever Vincenzo said to him was long and virulent and in Italian, and Helen had never before seen him so angry. What effect his words had on Guido would have been hard to guess, for that strong dark face showed only its most composed and confident expression, but Helen felt the passion that burned in him as strongly as if she had still been in touch with that hard vigorous body.

'Vincenzo, please!' Her voice was small and trembled slightly, but she stood her ground even when he turned on her with the fury still dark in his eyes.

'You left me,' he accused in a flat hard voice. 'You left me for Guido!'

'No, no, no, I *didn't*!' She glanced at Guido, but he seemed prepared to let her do it her way. 'Vincenzo, I got pulled into that—that crowd who were dancing, you know that, you saw it happen. Guido saw me and managed to pull me free of them, or I'd probably have been completely lost. I wouldn't have deliberately left you to go with Guido!'

'Guido!' He repeated the name with such venom that she shrank from it, shaking her head. 'This morning it was Signor Alessio, this evening it is Guido!'

'It is *festa*,' Guido pointed out with incredible coolness. 'Things are different for *festa*. Formalities are dropped and pretty girls are kissed, you know all this, Vincenzo, it is pointless to make such a *fracasso* about it!' He added something else in Italian, and whatever it was made Vincenzo turn and look at Helen again, with less of his first fury evident, but still with anger glittering deep in his eyes.

'So now you will come back to me, eh?' he asked, and shouted his anger when she automatically glanced at Guido before she answered him. 'I ask you, *ragazza*, not my brother! Do you look to him for permission?'

'Don't shout, Vincenzo!' Her own tension broke into anger at his bullying, and she caught a brief glimpse of a smile on Guido's sternly set mouth, she would have sworn it. Sticking out her chin, she faced Vincenzo, cheeks flushed and her eyes brightly gleaming. 'Yes, I'll come back with you, mostly because it wasn't your fault we got parted and you did bring me in the first place. But the fact that I've enjoyed myself for the last couple of hours or so is due to Guido— Signor Alessio, and I owe him my thanks.' She did not look at Guido while she said it, for his explanation still stuck in her mind, relentless as a probe, so cool and matter-of-fact. 'As he told you, this is *festa* and things are different. Bosses get called by their first names and girls get kissed. It's all part of the fun and nobody takes it seriously.'

Vincenzo was puzzled by her sudden anger, but Guido, she hoped, would think she resented being bullied for something she had no control over. Heaven forbid he should realise just how seriously she had taken his kiss just now, and she did not intend he should see how much his cool dismissal of it had affected her.

'Could we we go home now?' she asked in a small husky voice that, had she but known it, betrayed exactly how she felt. 'I'm not used to your Italian exuberance and I'm rather tired.' She turned to thank Guido, but did not look at him. 'Thank you, *signore*.'

'*Signorina*.' He took her hand in his hard, warm, brown fingers and raised it to his lips, a move so unexpected that she glanced up quickly and met the gleaming darkness of his eyes. 'Do not be too angry,' he murmured, and again pressed his mouth to her fingers. '*Buona notte,* Helen!'

He moved off down the sloping hill towards the emptying dance floor, and Vincenzo gave him time to get out of sight before he turned back to her. Slipping his hand under her arm, his eyes were once more a warm velvety brown. 'Come!' he said, and Helen obeyed silently. There was little point in doing anything else.

CHAPTER FOUR

DURING the week following the festival of Saint Catherine, Helen found herself thinking often about the necklace Guido had referred to as the Tears of Venus. Never had a piece of jewellery been so aptly named, she felt, for it resembled teardrops as nearly as it did raindrops, her original impression of it. Heaven knew why Guido had attached so much importance to whether or not she had seen her mysterious visitor wearing it, but it had seemed to matter to him at the time.

Ever since, she had been expecting him to follow up his interest, but he had said nothing more so far, nor was she any wiser regarding the identity of the mystery woman she had seen wearing the necklace. Guido obviously still considered it none of her business, as he had so bluntly remarked on the night of the festival.

Since the explosive scene between him and Vincenzo, she was even less inclined to say anything to Vincenzo about it too. For if he could react as he had that night to just one kiss during an event where it was a custom to kiss pretty girls, she dared not think what he would say about Guido being in her bedroom in the middle of the night, whatever the reason.

Such a lot had happened in the month she had been at the Villa Alessio that she sometimes wondered if she had become involved too deeply in the affairs of the Alessio family, and she gave a quite audible sigh when she anticipated how much more deeply she could get involved. Unconscious of having been overheard, she looked up and found Isabella's dark and frankly curious gaze on her.

'You are sad, *signorina*?' she asked. Never again since

the night of the festival had she used the more familiar
form of address, and Helen assumed it had been considered bad for discipline and therefore frowned upon.
'Are you bad friends with Tio Vincenzo?' Isabella insisted, and Helen smiled ruefully to herself.

Isabella would think of that, of course, and Helen
shook her head as she faced those huge and, at the
moment, very unchildlike eyes. Her pupil took a quite
embarrassing interest in her relationship with Vincenzo
and no amount of discouragement seemed to deter her.
'No, I haven't fallen out with your uncle,' Helen told
her, flicking over the pages of the book she was mark-
ing. 'I can't think what makes you say that.'

'Because you look sad and you sigh—so,' Isabella explained, and gave a very exaggerated impression of a
sigh. 'I thought it must be because you have quarrelled
with Tio Vincenzo.' No answer was forthcoming, but
Isabella did not give up so easily. Fine dark brows
arched and she regarded Helen from the corner of her
eye. 'Or is it that Papà has displeased you?' she guessed.

While admiring her persistence, Helen wished that
any change in her mood need not automatically be at-
tributed to either Guido or Vincenzo. 'I was simply
thinking about something, that's all,' she told Isabella.
'You shouldn't try to—analyse me, Isabella. It's very
embarrassing sometimes, and I wish you wouldn't do
it.'

'I am sorry.' Eyes downcast and her lower lip thrust
out, she looked a picture of injured innocence, so that
Helen barely restrained a smile. It was an old ploy and
one she was becoming more used to now. 'You are not
angry, *signorina*?'

'No, of course I'm not angry.' Helen put down the
book and looked across at her, amusement and resignation mingled in the smile she gave her. 'If you like, we
can walk down and see your father during our rest

period. If you're sure he won't mind us going while he's busy.'

'Oh no, he will not mind!' Isabella already had her book closed and was on her feet, smoothing down her dress and sparkling with excitement. She was always so easily roused to excitement and her huge eyes had such an extraordinary brilliance whenever it happened, that Helen sometimes felt she did not have sufficient outlet for her natural exuberance. 'He will be pleased to see us, *signorina*,' she promised, skipping with impatience. 'We have never been since you were here, not as we used to when Signora Billings was here. Do you not like horses, Signorina Purvis?'

The habit of visiting the stables with her governess was news to Helen, but she should not have been surprised, she supposed; Isabella would naturally be fond of horses. She shook her head over her own feelings about them. 'I haven't really thought about it,' she confessed. 'I've never been near a horse in my life, and I know nothing at all about them. They always *look* rather nice, but they're rather too big to take liberties with, I imagine.'

'Papà's horses are beautiful!' Isabella assured her with unconcealed pride. 'Most especially Venus d'Alessio, she is Papà's favourite and wins a lot of prizes for him. She is beautiful!'

Helen turned swiftly from checking her own reflection in a mirror and looked at her curiously. 'He has a horse called Venus?'

'A mare,' Isabella corrected her knowledgeably. 'Shiny like silk and chestnut-coloured. She was only very young when Papà bought her and he broke her himself; he says she is the most beautiful creature he has ever seen, that is why he called her Venus.'

Helen's smile was a little absent as she followed Isabella from the schoolroom. The Alessios had a penchant for the goddess of love, it seemed; they named not only their jewels after her but their horses too. It would be interesting to see what Guido considered the most beautiful creature he had ever seen, and she wondered idly if he included women in his judgment.

Outside, the late September sun touched everything with honey-gold, and yet again Helen feasted her eyes on the rich fertile countryside; it was something she never grew tired of. The stabling was built well away from the villa and on the topmost swell of the hill above Santa Caterina, dominating a landscape of vine-yards and olive groves, and dark-plumed clusters of cypresses. A small stream meandered downwards, glinting in the sunlight and occasionally leaping in minute waterfalls over the steeper parts of its route. The sky was still blue but a paler, less brilliant azure than when she first arrived.

Even in a month Helen felt she had developed a kind of affinity with this small corner of Tuscany, that she had felt for no other place. It had a warmth and a gen-erosity of nature that touched her heart and made her wish to stay there for ever, no matter how impractical the wish was.

Away from the shelter of the house and the gardens, the air was much cooler, and a light wind skimmed keenly over her bare arms, blowing her thin dress and moulding it to her body. Her hair, fine and pale in the sun, lifted from her neck and fluttered behind her as she narrowed her eyes against a sun that was still bright, although October was almost upon them.

Isabella led the way, naturally. Chattering inces-santly and always a step or two ahead, she danced im-patiently along beside the neat fencing that enclosed the practice arena, and Helen's heart began a more rapid beat as she followed her. She had never visited this part of the grounds before and she wished she had a more unbiassed authority on whether Guido was going to welcome their appearance.

Any moment now she would find out, for he was there in the ring, working the beautiful Venus d'Alessio, or so Isabella informed her as she stopped her dancing pace and climbed on to the fence to watch. Across on the far side, near the buildings, two men also leaned on the fence, critical eyes noting every move, and Helen could do no more than join Isabella, her interest caught at once by the combination of man and animal in perfect unison.

Isabella would have been quick to claim that he was the best in the world, and even Helen, who knew nothing about the sport, felt a thrill as she watched. They were a matchless pair and it seemed they knew it as well as the onlookers did, both man and horse performing with an arrogant confidence in their own perfection, and as they approached another fence, Helen caught her breath.

His hands forward on the mare's neck and the rein loose, Guido seemed to read the mind of his mount as she soared over the poles that looked much too high to Helen's inexperienced eye. But his head was up as she began the descent and he straightened his back, returning lightly to the saddle in time for a perfect landing, one hand letting go the rein for a congratulatory pat as they finished the circuit.

'He makes it look so easy,' Helen murmured, and Isabella looked at her confidently as they started once more along the path.

'To Papà it is easy,' she said. 'He is the best in the world.'

It was close enough, Helen thought, and allowed the boast to go unremarked. 'Do you ride, Isabella?' she asked, taking it for granted that she would, but Isabella shrugged her thin shoulders carelessly.

'I tried when I was much younger,' she admitted. 'But Papà said that I was too—hot-headed?—and he would not let me go on, even though Tio Vincenzo said I should.'

Hot-headed could well describe Isabella's occasional over-excitement, Helen thought, and decided the decision had probably been a wise one. Guido was obviously a good judge of his daughter's temperament, and he more than anyone knew the risks involved with a child who did not have sufficient control over her own moods, let alone those of an animal she was riding.

'You don't mind?' she asked, and Isabella again shrugged carelessly.

'No. I would much rather watch Papà than ride myself.'

By the time they arrived at the other side of the ring, practice was obviously finished for the moment, for one of the men who had been watching from the ringside was leading the mare away and Guido stood by the fence waiting for them to join him. He pulled off his peaked black velvet hat and brushed a forearm across his beaded forehead as Isabella went bounding up to him, garrulous and excited as a puppy.

'Shush, shush, shush!' He placed a finger over her lips to silence her, then lifted his daughter up on to the top rail of the fence, where she sat looking very pleased with herself and holding on to his shoulder for support. 'So,' he said, turning to Helen, 'Isabella has finally managed to persuade you down here?'

He leaned back against the fence, one hand holding Isabella's, and their faces quite close, making it easy to compare them. There was very little likeness to her father, Helen decided, even her eyes were brown and not black as Guido's were. In fact she was much more like Vincenzo than like her father, and she supposed it was as well, since, while his stunningly virile features were attractive in a man, they would be much less so in a girl.

'I wondered how long it would take her to lure you

here,' he went on. 'Do you not like horses, *signorina*?'

His current formality, she assumed, was for his daughter's benefit, and Helen laughed as she shook her head. 'Isabella asked me the same thing,' she told him, 'and I told her I'd never been near a horse in my life, I haven't any inhibitions either way. Anyway,' she added with a swift glance at his face, 'I wasn't sure if you welcomed visitors when you were practising.'

He regarded her for a moment, then eased his mouth into that shadow of a smile she remembered so well. 'There was one certain way to find out,' he told her. 'Isabella knows I have no objection to being watched, although I should draw the line at strangers, of course.'

There was something in the way he said that; something in the almost indolent softness of his voice that stirred responses in her she could not control. She was reminded again of a steep hillside above Santa Caterina and of the possessive strength of his arms around her, the hard fierceness of his mouth on hers.

'I—I didn't know,' she said, and hastily brought herself back to earth. 'You have an overseas event next month, haven't you? I think Isabella said it was in England, and I'm wondering if it would be very unpatriotic of me to wish you good luck.'

'It is an indoor event, quite an important one, as it happens.' He toyed with Isabella's thin childish fingers for a moment, not looking at Helen while he spoke. 'I suppose your loyalties are divided,' he guessed. 'In your heart you must support your own countrymen, but for appearances' sake, you feel you should wish *me* luck.'

Not only for appearances' sake, Helen thought, and the hasty way she avoided his eyes again must have made him wonder what he had said to bring that faint flush to her cheeks. 'But of course I wish you luck,' she insisted. 'Apart from anything else, Isabella would never forgive me if I didn't. Please give my love to London while you're there, won't you?'

'Yes, of course.' Black eyes scanned her face for a second. 'Do you miss it very much, Helen?'

'Not at all, to be quite honest!' She could truthfully tell him that because she felt she would miss this lush little corner of Italy more than she had missed London this past month. 'I've settled in quite happily here and I like it.'

'You are not homesick, or waiting for a holiday, so that you can go home?'

'Not at the moment,' she confessed. 'Although I expect I'll enjoy a holiday at home later on.'

'And when the *signorina* goes home for her holiday, she will be happy to take me too,' Isabella piped up quickly, her small face beaming with excitement. 'She will take me if you allow it, Papà! Will you agree? Will you let me go to England with Signorina Purvis?'

Helen's heart was hammering urgently, knowing how he was going to take this impulsive and unexpected request for his approval of something Isabella must know was bound to be refused as it had always been. She saw the look in Guido's eyes and Helen guessed he saw her as having put the idea into the child's head.

He turned and lifted Isabella down from the fence and put a hand on her smooth brown head for a moment. 'For the moment, *cara*,' he said gently, 'will you go and see that Luca is taking good care of Venus? I would like to speak with the *signorina* for a few moments.'

But deftly as he had handled it, Isabella was astute enough to know when she was being got rid of, and she must know too that it had something to do with her asking him to let Helen take her to England. She did as he asked, but she did it only reluctantly, and her dark eyes looked at Helen for a moment before she turned away. 'Sì, Papà.'

She might have been just about out of earshot when

Guido turned to Helen once more, but she must have heard the hardness in his voice even if she did not catch the words, because she glanced back over her shoulder and Helen saw her hesitate, her dark eyes anxious.

'You take too much upon yourself, *signorina*,' he said in the same flat harsh voice she had heard him use before when he was angry. 'You should not make promises that you cannot keep, and especially to a child. Have you no conscience? Do you not care that she will be upset when she learns that she cannot go with you?'

Helen flushed. She was uncertain which had precedence at the moment, anger or hurt, but she was appalled to realise just how much this man could affect her. She should be capable of turning on him and telling him the truth without wanting to burst into tears at the same time because he had misjudged her. Instead she was still without words when he went on, apparently never doubting for a moment she was in the wrong.

'You will do me the favour of not mentioning the idea to Isabella ever again,' he insisted, 'and perhaps she may forget in time. You must realise how irresponsible you were to make such a promise without first consulting me.'

'But I *didn't*!'

Tapping the cane he carried, in a sharp tattoo against one leg, he regarded her steadily, until he caught sight of Isabella coming back from the stable, her mission apparently completed. She would be uneasy, Helen guessed, and noticed Guido's frown, as if he had more to say and needed more time to say it.

Seeing his time limited, he was impatient and he kept an eye on his daughter as she came back towards them, kicking up small clods of earth with her toes and watching them closely, defiantly. 'Papà,' she called, as if to warn him of her approach, 'it is all right. Venus is being groomed and Luca is taking good care of her.'

'*Bene!*' He turned back swiftly to Helen. 'This is not the time or the place,' he decreed, 'but I will speak with you privately, *signorina*, later today. After dinner in my office perhaps, when Isabella is in bed.'

It was not so much a request as a command, and Helen marvelled at how quickly situations could change. Only a week ago she had stood with this same man on a moonlit hill and thrilled to the touch of that hard mouth, been caressed by the black eyes that now glittered at her so relentlessly.

'If you say so, *signore*,' she said in a small, tight and very unsteady voice. 'You *are* my employer, I can hardly refuse!'

She said it with a certain air of bravado, and noticed how he lifted his head and looked down his autocratic nose at her. 'As you say, *signorina*! I am glad that you remember it sometimes!' Ignoring her swift flush, he turned to his daughter. 'Did I not say that I wished to speak with Signorina Purvis, Isabella?' he asked her, and she nodded. But the way she thrust out her bottom lip reminded Helen of Vincenzo being reproachful.

'Yes, Papà.'

Isabella's eyes were huge and she looked from one to the other anxiously. She was intelligent enough to know that she had been the cause of her father's sudden anger and of Helen's unhappy look, and it was possible she regretted her own impulsiveness as much as anyone. But however much he blamed Helen, it was clear that he attached no blame at all to his daughter.

'I think it is time you returned to your books, *cara*, hmm?' he suggested. Drawing her against him, he stroked her hair, bending to kiss the top of her head and rest his cheek for a moment on her shiny crown. 'Recreation time is over, *piccola*.'

He loves her, Helen thought, and found her own anger diminished by the knowledge. He loves her desperately, and he acts as if he's afraid of losing her, which was ridiculous. Inevitably, she thought about Isabella's mother again; the woman whom no one had ever mentioned except Isabella herself. Guido's mystery wife, whose daughter did not even know for sure what nationality she was.

Just as inevitably she recalled the ghostly white figure in her room that Guido had tried so hard to convince her was merely a figment of her imagination. He had never openly admitted her existence, even when he had questioned Helen about whether or not she was wearing the necklace he referred to as the Tears of Venus, and somewhere in the back of her mind was the niggling, disturbing suspicion that the two women were one and the same. It was a suspicion that Helen always thrust hastily away, but there was so much she did not know or understand about Guido Alessio, and deep in her heart she admitted an ever growing need to understand him.

Helen had disliked telling Vincenzo that she could not spend the rest of the evening with him once dinner was finished, because she had been ordered, there was no other phrase for it, to see Guido in his office. She hadn't told him the subject of the reprimand she expected, but merely said it was a matter of policy concerning Isabella's lessons. Whatever the reason, Vincenzo was annoyed enough to declare himself ready to go himself and tell Guido exactly what he thought of him encroaching into her free time. It had taken all her persuasive powers to talk him out of it.

Helen had half hoped that Guido would forget about the interview, but a brief and unmistakable glance as they left the dinner-table warned her that it was a vain hope. After dinner she and Isabella had played card games until Isabella's bedtime, and when she was gone Helen gave Vincenzo a brief resigned shrug and made her way along to Guido's private sanctum at the rear of the house.

She hesitated a second, trying to do something about the wild, breathtaking beat of her heart, then she knocked lightly, half hoping there would be no answer. But the firm deep voice was unmistakable and she noted too that he used Italian and not English when he bade her come in.

'*Avanti!*'

She obeyed the summons warily, and the angle of her chin could have left him in little doubt that she resented being called over the coals like a naughty schoolgirl. 'I've come as instructed,' she told him in a not quite steady voice. 'Although you made your feelings perfectly plain, Signor Alessio, however misguided they are. I wouldn't have thought it was necessary to—rub it in!'

The light grey suit he wore added height and leanness to an already impressive body, and she noticed he had dispensed with the tie he had worn at dinner. The neck of a pale blue shirt showed a plunge of bronzed skin as far as the first shadow of dark hair on his chest, and her eye was drawn inevitably to that small pulsing spot at the base of his throat. It was always startling to recognise just how he could affect her, and Helen felt resentment of the fact in this instance as she never had before.

'Please sit down, Helen.'

His quietness and the use of her first name disarmed her in the first instance, and then made her more wary, so that she eyed him suspiciously as she sat down on the comfortable chair he assigned her to. 'If I'm to be put in my place again,' she said in a very uncertain voice, 'I'm not sure I wouldn't rather be on my feet. Especially when you're still standing!'

In fact he was sat on the edge of the desk, on the same side as she was, and she found his proximity too disturbing to accept willingly. He leaned back and took a strong black Tuscan cigar from a box and lit it, eyeing her for a moment through the smoke of it before he said anything. 'You have no need to be so determinedly aggressive,' he told her, in a tone that brought a swift flush to her cheeks. 'I merely wish to discover exactly what was said about Isabella going to England with you. You have denied that you made such a promise, I know, but I find it difficult to believe that Isabella herself could have simply—dreamed up the idea. Are you telling me that she deliberately lied about you having discussed it with her?'

Her immediate concern was with Isabella, and she hesitated to be as specific as he obviously expected. 'I'm not saying that she deliberately lied,' she said, 'but I think she took matters a little further in her imagination than they went in fact. And also wishful thinking has a great deal to do with it.'

'Tell me what *did* happen,' he insisted. 'Was the matter discussed or not?'

In the circumstances Helen found it impossible to remain seated, so she got to her feet and paced restlessly across to the window, casting him a brief, wary glance as she passed him. Having put some distance between them, she turned to face him again, with the light of the window behind her. 'There isn't much to tell,' she told him. 'Isabella wanted to know something about England, and I told her about London and about Surrey, the only two places I know really well. Then she said she was always asking you or Vincenzo to take her to England, and that neither of you would.'

He swore softly in Italian and frowned at the toes of his shoes instead of looking at her, so that Helen began to wonder if he was at last going to explain something about Isabella's mysterious mother. 'It is not in her best interests at the moment, for a very good reason. A reason I do not have to explain to you,' he added quickly, as if he suspected she was about to ask him.

'But I must insist that you do not encourage this—this dream of hers. Do you understand?'

'Not in the least!' Helen told him, and refused to be intimidated by the swift drawing of his black brows. 'But I'll abide by your decision, of course, since you're her father. Only what do I say to her if she asks me again about taking her with me?'

'You simply say that you cannot take her!' Guido said firmly. 'No good will come of discussing it, and I do not want the subject mentioned ever again.'

Helen looked at him in despair, wondering how he could seem so uncaring when she knew very definitely that he wasn't. 'Can't you just take her once?' she pleaded, heedless of the tight line his mouth made in that boldly imperious face. 'Her mother was English, and perhaps——'

'How did you know that?' The demand was swift and so angry that for a moment Helen stared at him uncomprehendingly. 'Who told you that Isabella's mother was English?' he went on relentlessly. 'Vincenzo? What else has he confided to you, Helen, eh? How many more of our family affairs have been aired for your entertainment?'

'None at all!' Helen's heart beat so hard that it almost choked her, and she groped behind her for the support of a small table that stood in the window. He was on his feet too now, and looking across at her with burning black eyes that seemed to accuse her of heaven knew what, and made her tremble like a leaf. 'You accuse me without a shred of evidence for what you're saying!' she charged angrily. 'Vincenzo has never told me anything about you or your family, and I've certainly never asked! It was Isabella herself who told me she thought her mother must have been English because she's being taught to be so—so English! Naturally she's curious—any ten-year-old child would be!'

Guido drew deeply on the cigar and expelled a thick

cloud of pungent smoke. 'Her mother is dead,' he said with stark frankness. 'There is no use in looking for her.'

Helen had known it was more than likely, of course, and yet she still could not dissociate Isabella's mother from the woman she had seen in her room. Or she could not dissociate Guido's wife from the mystery woman, perhaps that was the answer. Perhaps they were not the same woman, it would at least account for the mystery surrounding Isabella's mother, and for Guido's almost over-protective attitude towards his daughter.

'I'm sorry,' she said, rousing herself from speculation. 'I didn't know, of course, but——'

'There is a great deal you do not know, nor need to know,' he interrupted harshly. 'And you would do well not to involve yourself in matters that do not concern you. You were engaged as Isabella's governess, and that is the extent of your interest—remember it!'

'Oh, I will, *signore*, I'm fully aware of my standing!'

Her voice trembled and she felt much too close to tears for her own peace of mind. But something urged her on; some need to strike back at him for the hurt he could inflict by so firmly and consistently reminding her that she was merely his employee and nothing more. When he so determinedly denied her an interest in his daughter's welfare and sought to put her so firmly in her place, she wished she could dislike him; hate was out of the question because it involved passion and such thoughts were dangerous where Guido was concerned. So instead she tried to prick him with her anger.

'The trouble is I find it hard to keep pace with your requirements!' she told him huskily. 'First you tried to convince me I'd dreamed the woman I saw in my bedroom that night, then you went to a lot of trouble to make me remember whether or not that figment of my imagination had been wearing a necklace you were interested in! I'll try not to remember how impressively you apologised for bullying me too, because you had a glib answer for that, of course; it was *festa*!' She caught her breath in her throat so that it sounded very like a sob. 'Just—forgive me if I find it a little difficult to remember my place occasionally, that's all, *signore*!'

'Helen!'

There was a note of warning in his voice, but something else too. A suggestion of huskiness that she had noticed when he stood with her in her bedroom that night, and again on the hill above Santa Caterina, and she shivered. 'I'd feel much more sure of where I stand if you called me just plain *signorina*, or perhaps Signorina Purvis, when you're feeling very formal,' Helen told him, shakily defiant. 'It would serve to remind me of my place and I wouldn't be always forgetting!'

'Stop it, damn you!' He came across to her in long angry strides, his eyes glittering. 'That is *enough*!'

'More than enough, I agree!' Helen concurred. 'It may not have occurred to you, Signor Alessio, but I don't like being accused of gossiping about my employer, or of priming my pupil to ask embarrassing questions of her father!'

'But you must also agree,' Guido interrupted firmly, 'that I have the right to discover why Isabella is suddenly so sure I will let her go to England with you. If you assure me that you did not do so, then I accept your word.'

But he was not going to apologise, Helen realised, and for a moment fought desperately with a desire to demand that he did. Instead she put her feelings into words he could not fail to understand, and could only pray that he was not completely untouched by the threat she issued. 'I've grown fond of Isabella,' she told him, firmly controlling her voice, 'and I think she likes me. But if you're going to constantly question my motives like this, then I shall have no alternative but to return to England, much as I'd hate to leave Isabella. I can't stand being always under suspicion! The next thing I know is that something will go missing and I shall be accused of stealing it! I seem to be your first——'

'*Dio mio!*' His fingers dug bruisingly hard into her arms and he shook her hard. 'What are you talking about? Tell me what you mean by that, *mia ragazza*, before I shake it from you!'

Stunned and breathless, Helen tried to fight him off with clenched hands, pounding at the broad unyielding chest and wriggling desperately. 'Let me go!' she panted. 'Let me go, Guido, you're hurting me!'

He let go one arm and grasped her chin instead, forcing her to look at him. Her eyes were bright and glistening with angry tears and she was breathing hard, a furious mingling of emotions depriving her of rational thought, for he was much too close and her body responded to the angry vigour of his in a way she could not control.

When he spoke again it was in his own tongue initially, and then in English that was more strongly accented than usual, but his voice was less harsh and his anger slightly diminished, it seemed. 'What makes you speak of stealing?' he demanded. 'Tell me!'

Helen was not even sure herself; she had spoken impulsively, and in anger, without any foundation for what she said, and she shook her head slowly, stunned by his reaction, and uneasy too. 'I don't know,' she whispered. 'I just—I just said it, that's all.'

'You just said——'

They both turned quickly when someone pounded hard on the office door, and Vincenzo's voice called through the heavy wooden panels, thick with suspicion. 'Helen? Are you still there?'

It was just possible he had been waiting out there for her and had heard her cry out, but more likely he was simply impatient because she had been with Guido for so long. Passing her tongue swiftly across her lips, Helen glanced at Guido before she answered.

'I'll be out in a minute, Vincenzo!' Then turning back to Guido she brushed a hand over slightly dishevelled hair and met his eyes for only a moment. 'I don't know what you have in mind, Signor Alessio,' she said in a small and very unsteady voice, 'but obviously, and inevitably, you suspected the worst. *Is* something missing?' She thought she detected a slight change in his expression and her throat constricted, making her swallow hard. 'It's all right,' she told him, 'you needn't tell me it's not my concern, I know that tune by heart now!'

The door panels resounded again to Vincenzo's fist. 'Helen!'

He was not the most patient of men, and if no one answered he would quite likely come charging in without invitation. But before she could reply to the latest assault on the door, Guido forestalled her, sharply and impatiently. '*Aspetti*, Vincenzo! *Dannazione, ella viene! Aspetti!*'

He did not take his eyes off her even while he was telling his brother to wait, she was coming, and Helen realised with dismay that she was trembling. The compelling nearness of him was disturbing her self-possession as always, but hard as it was to do she looked up at him and angled her chin slightly, finding the challenge irresistible.

'Is there any reason for me to stay any longer?' she asked. 'Are you in fact going to charge me with stealing something?'

He rolled his big hands into fists and for a moment Helen feared he would actually strike her, for his eyes blazed furiously and the lean length of him shivered with angry passion. 'Damn you, Helen!' he rasped harshly.

It was curious how little satisfaction it gave her to have scored off him, and she looked at him for only a second or two before lowering her eyes. 'Vincenzo's getting impatient,' she reminded him, and added with no thought of being deliberately provocative, 'You don't want me for anything else, do you, *signore*?'

For a moment the very air between them shivered with violence, and her hands clasped tightly together kept them from trembling visibly. Her mouth was soft and quiveringly unsteady and when he moved a half-step closer the vibrance of him kindled the same wild, uncontrollable desires in her, her skin tingling with his warmth. A hand reached out and lightly touched her arm, then was withdrawn with obvious reluctance when Vincenzo's fist pounded once more on the door.

Turning abruptly from her, Guido walked across to his desk, his hands riffling through the papers there. 'No,' he said without looking at her again, 'there is nothing else I want you for. *Buona notte!*'

Helen did not move immediately because she found it hard to bring her shaking legs under control, and she brushed traces of tears from her eyes with a finger-tip while she looked across at that strong, unfathomable profile. 'Goodnight,' she murmured huskily, and went out to join Vincenzo. Guido, she noticed when she turned to close the door, did not even turn his head.

CHAPTER FIVE

ISABELLA made no mention of the forbidden subject the following morning and Helen assumed that she too had had the situation firmly spelled out to her by her father. It would account for the slight downward droop of her mouth and the absence of her customary smile, and Helen wondered if, even now, Guido fully appreciated just how much that longed for trip to England meant to his daughter. Not for anything would she deliberately defy him and try to explain to Isabella why she couldn't give the promise she had done her best to extract, but she wished she could have said something to console her.

Even with the schoolroom windows closed the morning was cooler and, although Isabella seemed not to notice it as she bent industriously over an essay she had been set, Helen shivered at the chilliness of her bare arms. Glancing across at Isabella, she got up from her desk. 'I'm not very warm,' she explained when the girl looked up for a moment, 'so I'm going to fetch a jacket from my room, Isabella. I won't be a minute, just carry on with your essay until I come back. O.K.?'

Isabella nodded without speaking, and when she bowed her head over her exercise book once more, Helen pulled a rueful face. Obviously, however kindly Guido had explained the situation, his daughter had not found it easy to accept, and she was showing her displeasure very pointedly. But knowing Isabella as she did, Helen was not unduly worried, for she would more than likely be her usual sunny and irrepressible self by lunchtime.

Quietly closing the schoolroom door behind her,

Helen made her way upstairs, momentarily thoughtful as she turned along the gallery, and she brought up sharply when she realised someone was in the act of leaving her bedroom. She stopped dead in her tracks and stared, her heart thudding hard, not simply because a stranger had been into her bedroom, but because there was something disturbingly familiar about the intruder.

As she watched, too startled to move, the tall figure of a woman began to walk away from her along the gallery, a pale green housecoat flowing around her as she went, and reminding Helen of another image still lodged irremovably in her mind's eye. This was no ethereal shape seen through a mirror in the shadowy deception of moonlight, and the garment she wore was not a ghostly white gown, but Helen was convinced she was seeing her nocturnal visitor again, and her reaction was one not only of alarm but indecision.

Here was proof for her own eyes that the intruder was a flesh and blood woman and not a figment of her sleep-befuddled brain as Guido had implied, and she did not quite know what to do about it. In the event, the need for decision was taken out of her hands, for it was almost as if the laboured thudding of her heart was audible; the woman turned suddenly and looked at her.

In the perennial dusk of the gallery Helen saw her clearly for the first time and was able to distinguish features, for the woman was coming back towards her, with the pale housecoat fluttering in a breeze of her own creating. Soft-footed and so far silent, almost as alarming to Helen's uncertain mind, as on their first encounter.

She was rather older than Helen expected, possibly in her middle forties, but she still had an exceptional kind of beauty, with smooth cameo-like features. Her hair was long and black, but it had a fine mesh of silver in its darkness, and her skin had the translucent pallor of the permanent invalid. It was the eyes, however, that made most impression on Helen, and it took her only a moment to realise why it was.

Initially they reminded her of Isabella's and Vincenzo's. They were huge in a rather small face, just as Isabella's were, and a soft velvety brown, but they had a curious blankness as they peered at her from below drawn black brows, and Helen's pulse fluttered a warning. There was no bright, alert intelligence behind these eyes, and the lack of it gave their beauty a hauntingly lost look that was somehow chilling.

'*Chi è lei?*' she asked in a thin voice. '*Chi è lei, signorina? Non la conosco!*'

Helen could guess she was being asked to identify herself, but she was still trying to cope with something she found very hard to accept. Those curiously blank eyes troubled her, and caused little shivers to flutter over her skin. 'I'm sorry,' she said, and only just stopped herself from taking a backward step when the woman leaned towards her. 'I don't speak Italian. Do— do you speak any English?'

'*L'inglese?*' The frown deepened and the silver-streaked head shook rapidly back and forth in agitation. '*No, no, no, non capisco! Parla l'italiano!*'

Helen shrugged helplessly. Normally the problem of language could be easily overcome with a little ingenuity, but this situation had little to do with normality and she felt another flutter of apprehension. Along at the end of the gallery was the door that she had seen Guido close so carefully behind him that night, and it seemed fairly obvious that the woman before her was normally confined to that room. Helen's wish at the moment was to return her to it with as little fuss as possible, for she felt sure that Guido would dislike her making this discovery more than anything she had done so far.

It took all her tact and persuasion, and completely exhausted her meagre knowledge of Italian, so diligently learned over the weeks, to persuade the woman to go back along the gallery. But eventually she achieved it, and accompanied her as far as the door just to be sure, regretting all the time the impulse that had sent her in search of something to cover her arms.

The room door stood wide open and her companion brushed past her, a thin hand briefly in contact with Helen's arm and raising the chill of goose-flesh. But it was not to be as simple as that, for when Helen would have drawn back the same hand clamped about her arm and drew her into the room, and such an invitation was difficult to refuse.

It was not simply a bedroom, Helen realised, but a luxuriously furnished sitting-room and more than likely part of a suite of rooms, for several more doors opened off and suggested a self-contained unit. It would explain why this strange, unworldly woman was so seldom seen outside her own sanctum, and how her presence in the household went virtually unnoticed. It was the fact of her being kept so strictly secret, however, that Helen found most disturbing.

'Signorina?'

Caught unawares, Helen swung round quickly, her look of surprise so easy to mistake for guilt as she stared at the woman who came through one of the other doors. So much for her hope of leaving before anyone else realised she had been there—and she thought specifically of Guido; but it was too late now. All she wished was that she need not feel so alarmingly guilty about being discovered.

Heart drumming anxiously, she watched a short, thickset woman come quickly across the room. Small black eyes darted suspiciously at Helen, but at the same time she crooned softly to the woman beside her, until the grip on Helen's arm eased and finally fell away. In her relief she would have fled quickly from an increasingly bizarre situation, but for something she heard suddenly among the lyrical babble of Italian.

Unmistakably the new arrival had addressed the woman beside her as Signora Alessio, and suddenly it seemed her worse suspicions had been confirmed. Her legs felt alarmingly weak and she needed a few moments to come to terms with the fact that everything pointed to the likelihood of the mystery woman being Guido's wife after all.

So many times she had admitted the possibility, but without any real conviction, and now she was faced with it as a reality she found it incredibly hard to accept. She had not until now considered a reason for her being hidden away in the room at the end of the gallery. She had certainly never anticipated anyone like this blank-eyed shell of a beauty, helpless as a child and some ten years Guido's senior.

With comforting arms and a gentle hand the older woman soothed the silvery dark head as she led her charge across to an armchair and saw her seated in it before she looked up again at Helen, still standing dazed and only half believing by the door. The small suspicious eyes were set in a round brown countrywoman's face, and they were fiercely possessive, resentful and distrustful.

'You will go now, *signorina*,' she said in passable English, and with a definite air of authority. 'I will care for the *signora*.'

Helen's tongue flicked anxiously across dry lips as she sought to justify her being there, and she lingered despite her anxiety to leave. 'I came in because I found——'

'*Sì, sì*, is all right!'

Her explanation was cut short and it was clear from those dark unfriendly eyes that the woman was anxious to be rid of her, so that Helen hesitated no longer.

Turning swiftly, she went out on to the gallery once more and as she pulled the door closed behind her, she brushed a trembling hand over her forehead and found it beaded with moisture. She had taken no more than a single step when she heard something that made her blood run cold and sent her spinning round quickly to stare at the closed door. For unmistakably she had heard a key turn in the lock.

She almost ran back downstairs and completely forgot about the jacket she had gone for, her stunned senses coping with a tumult of emotions she tried hard to subdue. Who should she feel most sorry for? That haunting-eyed beauty up there, or Guido who had tried so hard to deny her existence? She was so distracted that she hurried almost blindly down the wide staircase and saw and heard nothing until someone spoke her name suddenly.

'Helen?'

Startled, she turned too quickly and missed her footing, stumbling clumsily down the last few steps and trying in vain to snatch a hold on the balustrade to save herself. Instead of suffering a fall, however, she was caught in a pair of enveloping arms and held close for a moment to a stunningly familiar maleness that started her pulses racing. Never before had she felt guilty about being in his arms, but she clung to the excuse of her fall to keep contact with him as long as possible.

Guido held her for a moment with her face pressed to the thudding beat of his heart, then he eased her away and looked down into her face, a scrutiny which she hastily avoided. He wore a cream shirt that emphasised his bronzed skin, and felt smooth and soft under her hands, his warmth mingling with the familiar scents of tobacco and the inescapable tang of the stable. There was an earthy, sensual excitement about being in his arms that never failed to stir her to a response, but in this instance she fought more anxiously than ever to subdue it.

'Did I startle you so much?' he asked, and when she again avoided his eyes, he slid a hand beneath her chin and raised her face to him. Glancing behind her up the empty staircase, he arched a black brow curiously. 'Is there something wrong, Helen? You look—distinctly uneasy, and I cannot imagine why.'

'No reason,' she assured him quickly. It was too soon after seeing that poor soul upstairs and hearing her called Signora Alessio to be reconciled to the fact of her very likely being Guido's wife, and she made a move to free herself. Reaching down, she put her own hands over the ones still at her waist, breaking their hold and stepping back, but brought up short by the bottom step. 'I felt rather cold, so I went for a cardigan from my——'

She stopped when he took obvious note of her bare arms, and realised for the first time that she had never completed her original errand. 'It seems you no longer feel so cold,' Guido observed quietly. 'Can it be that something has happened to make you feel much warmer suddenly?'

He was looking at her with his black gaze deep and unwavering, unnerving in its intensity, and Helen wondered what was going on in his mind. 'I—something happened, I stopped to speak to someone and—well, I forgot about my jacket. I was sidetracked, I didn't realise.' She stumbled over her explanation and knew from the way he was looking at her that her obvious edginess was making him suspicious.

'Where is Isabella?'

The enquiry was inevitable and Helen answered it without hesitation. 'She's all right, I left her writing an essay, it's something she can quite easily do unsupervised.'

'While you interest yourself elsewhere, it seems,' Guido said.

Helen flushed, unwilling to tell him where she had been but wanting to put him right about her motives. 'I haven't been gone very long,' she protested. 'You have no cause to look at me like that!'

'It makes you feel uneasy?'

His voice was soft—too soft, Helen thought, and hastened to defend herself. 'Why should I feel uneasy?' she asked. 'I haven't a conscience about anything, if that's what you're implying. I was delayed and I forgot my cardigan, that's all—I've committed no crime!'

'And you did not know that Vincenzo was home, of course!' said Guido, and she stared at him, taken unaware.

She had no idea that Vincenzo was home, but it would account for his suspicion, of course, and she flushed indignantly at the idea of his thinking her guilty of trying to deceive him. 'As it happens I *didn't* know,' she insisted, and his eyes narrowed.

'So?' That maddening comment on anything and everything that he used with such effect made her clench her hands tightly. 'I saw him go upstairs only about fifteen minutes ago.'

'Then I haven't been very long in the circumstances, have I?' she retorted defiantly, and he said something low and virulent in his own tongue, his eyes hard as jet.

'If I find I was correct in my first impression,' he said in a hard flat voice, 'you know what I threatened to do! I do not like to think I have been wrong about you, Helen, but if you——'

'If you're thinking I've been with Vincenzo for the past quarter of an hour, you can think again!' Helen declared, and she let out her breath in a slow soft growl of exasperation. 'Oh, you just don't trust anybody, do you?' She hastily avoided his eyes, but stuck to her guns. 'You owe me an apology, though I haven't much hope that you'll make it!'

He blocked her way and she could not bring herself yet to brush past him and go back to the schoolroom, but she looked beyond him to where the outside door stood half open, and sighed inwardly for the opportunity to escape into the open air. 'If I am wrong, then I apologise.' She snatched her gaze back swiftly and looked up at him, trying to fathom those dark, fathomless eyes. 'If not Vincenzo, then who delayed you, Helen?'

Fearful that even by looking at her he would know she had been to that room at the end of the gallery, she made an attempt to dodge past him, but he snatched at her arm as she brushed against him, and held it firm. 'Guido! Please!'

Her voice was no more than a whisper and she glanced up the stairs behind her, afraid that Vincenzo might come and find them. 'You will go when I say you may!' he told her harshly. 'I have not yet finished with you, *mia ragazza*! Who have you seen that distracted you so much you forgot to bring the jacket you needed?'

'No one!'

'You lie, Helen!' He spoke softly and her whole body shivered in response. His long hard fingers interlaced with hers and he held her hand against his heart so that its steady pulse beat against her palm. 'Who else could bring such a flush of colour to your cheeks and make you forget the reason you left the schoolroom?'

'Please don't!'

Her position was impossible, and she felt her own heart thudding in anxiety lest she give herself away. She felt he would rather she had been with his brother than know that she had learned who it was in that secret room, kept under lock and key; it was something he would hate her, or anyone outside his family, to know. And knowing the kind of man he was, knowing

how virile and passionate he could be, she could pity
him with such a wife. Only in this instance pity could
come dangerously close to love, and that was more unthinkable than ever now.

Her sudden move took him by surprise. Wrenching
her arm free, she darted past him and went hurrying
across the hall towards the schoolroom, breathing hard
and trying to control her shaking legs. Behind her she
heard the scrape of his booted feet on the tile surround,
and her heart almost stopped beating. Then his voice
carried clear and strong in the wake of her flight.

'Helen!'

She did not stop to consider whether it was anger or
pleading that gave the cry that sharp edge, but she ignored it, even though she knew she could well be bringing about her own dismissal by doing so. To her relief
he did not catch up with her and she brushed an unexpected tear from her lashes as she opened the schoolroom door.

Another door, across the hall and leading out into
the garden, slammed shut in the same instant and she
looked across to where he had been standing. Solving
the mystery of her nocturnal visitor had brought her no
satisfaction at all, only a frightening realisation of why
Guido guarded his private affairs so fiercely, and the
knowledge that while that blank-eyed beauty lived, he
was completely unattainable.

Helen ate very little at lunch time, and she was aware
all through the meal of Guido's black-eyed gaze on her,
though she affected not to notice and chatted with
Vincenzo with a rather forced gaiety. Following custom, the lunch break was a fairly long one, and when
they had finished eating, she and Vincenzo took a stroll
around the garden as they often did.

Today she was more than ever thankful for his company, for she felt certain that had she been alone Guido

would have insisted on taking up that fiery argument again. Even so her unaccustomed preoccupation was noticeable, and Vincenzo eyed her curiously once or twice, but had so far said nothing.

At a curve in the stone-paved path, where the shrubs grew thickly but not high enough to hide the upper windows of the house from view, he stopped walking and took her in his arms. He held her for a moment without saying anything, just smiling and quizzing her with his soft brown eyes, and almost inevitably Helen found herself comparing the sensation of being in his arms with that of being in Guido's embrace.

It was pleasant enough, but there was not the same thrill of excitement, and the realisation of how deeply Guido could affect her frightened her for a moment and made her wonder what she would do if ever she fell deeply in love with him. Whatever happened she must never allow herself to get too close to him again, no matter how difficult it might prove.

'*Mia bella* Elena.' Vincenzo pressed his cheek to hers and murmured the words against her ear. The lyrical Italian version of her name was a familiar ploy of Vincenzo's when he had seduction in mind, and today Helen was slightly more willing to succumb than she usually was, if only to banish the remembered strength of Guido's arms and the warm virility of his body. '*Molta bella, carissima,*' Vincenzo whispered huskily. 'Kiss me, *cara mia.*'

Helen lifted her face to him and she yielded to the ardent strength of his arms about her, but her senses refused to respond, however willing she told herself she was. For the moment Vincenzo seemed not to notice it and he snuggled his face against her neck, murmuring softly in his own tongue, his voice muffled by her hair and kissing her lightly between each word, but she felt little of the pleasure it normally gave her.

Instead she opened her eyes and found her gaze

drawn to the upper windows of the villa, visible above the surrounding shrubs. While Vincenzo sought a more passionate response from her, she watched the glint of the October sun on the tall panes and felt a little of the sadness of autumn touch her susceptible heart. Then she caught a glimpse of movement behind one of them. An impression of a pale oval face amid cloudy dark hair and of pale draperies that was no more than a moment before it was gone.

His mouth close to her ear and nibbling gently at the lobe, Vincenzo knew nothing of what she saw, only felt the slight tension in her body when she caught her breath. When he raised his head and looked down into her face there was a hazy warmth in his eyes and that sensual lower lip, shared by all the Alessio men, was thrust out in a knowing smile.

'What is wrong, *carissima*?' he murmured, then kissed her long and lingeringly on her mouth. But Helen was now even less in tune with his mood and his frown, when he looked down at her again, gave an indication of his disappointment. 'Helen! You are not with me in mind, are you?'

The strangeness of her own mood troubled her and she wanted nothing so much as to shake it off. Lifting her arms, she encircled his neck and smiled up at him, a vaguely apologetic smile that did not reach her eyes. 'I'm sorry, Vincenzo, I'm afraid I'm *not* really with you.'

'I have noticed,' he said with a hint of irony, and tipped up her chin, looking down at her mouth with an expression that would at any other time have sent shivers of pleasure slipping along her spine. 'I think you are—concerned about something,' he went on, but from his expression it was clear he did not consider it anything very serious. 'All through lunch you chattered desperately, even though Guido was watching you with his most baleful look, which makes me suspect that he is the cause of your—absence of mind.' He clasped both his hands behind her in the small of her back and looked at her coaxingly, mouth pursed and his eyes hooded with half-lids and heavy lashes. 'Tell me what troubles you, *bella mia*, and I will make it right for you; I will scold Isabella if she is the cause, or even thrash Guido if I have to. *Là!*'

Helen smiled at his extravagance and felt thankful for his open, uncomplicated nature. Vincenzo was unlikely to have secrets to hide, although inevitably he must know of Signora Alessio, and it was she who was uppermost in Helen's mind at the moment. She had never said a word to Vincenzo about that night, but now she felt herself compelled by something she could no longer control, though she still would keep Guido's visit to her room from him.

'I never told you about my ghostly visitor, did I?' she asked, and knew from the sudden curious stillness of him that he was already preparing to tread cautiously. 'I woke in the middle of the night one time, just after I came here, and thought I saw a ghost in my bedroom.'

His momentary hesitation told its own story, and she waited. 'You had a bad dream, *dolce mia*,' he said eventually. 'There is no *spettro* here.'

Helen was prepared for him to follow his brother's line and she was shaking her head firmly. 'No, it wasn't a dream, Vincenzo,' she told him, quietly insistent. 'I was awake and I saw her. I know she wasn't a ghost either, because I went out on to the gallery not long afterwards and Guido was just closing the door of the room at the end of the gallery.' She glanced obliquely at his smooth handsome features. 'I'd always thought those rooms were unoccupied.'

'Guido was probably restless,' he suggested without confirming the fact that the end room was unoccupied, then he smiled at her a little crookedly. 'Or maybe he also saw your ghost, eh?'

'I'm convinced he did,' she said, and ignored the warning voice in her brain that warned her how much Guido would dislike this present conversation. He would say that she was yet again concerning herself with matters that were nothing to do with her, and it was probably true, but she had come too far now to go back. 'Guido *is* angry with me,' she confessed, and looked up appealingly at him. 'He's angry because I daren't tell him where I'd been when he saw me coming downstairs in the middle of the morning. He said you were home, and he thought—he suspected I'd been with you.'

Vincenzo's clasped hands pressed her hard against him, and there was a wistfulness in his voice that she knew stemmed not only from the words he spoke. 'I wish that you had been, *carissima*, but I am not so fortunate, eh?'

He was as unwilling to talk about her as Guido had been, she sensed, but with Vincenzo she could say what she dared not say to Guido. 'I saw Signora Alessio, Vincenzo.'

'*Madre di Dio!*' Vincenzo murmured, and she hurried on.

'She'd been into my room again, Vincenzo, I saw her coming out and she turned and saw me, and spoke to me. I didn't understand her because she apparently doesn't speak English, but she let me take her back to her room eventually, and then she wouldn't let me go. If someone hadn't come——'

'Guido?'

He asked the question anxiously, and Helen shook her head, recalling her own relief at that. 'No, it was an elderly woman. Someone I've never seen before.'

'Her name is Teresa Pucelli,' Vincenzo said. 'She has been with Violante for a long time and guards her diligently.'

'Violante?'

He didn't reply to that, but half-turned his head and darted a swift look over his shoulder at the row of windows. Then he kissed her in a curiously light and absent way, as if he did it automatically, and turned her into the crook of his arm as he started back to the house. They had walked some distance before he said anything more.

'It was this that you did not wish to tell Guido?' he asked, and Helen nodded. 'Because?' he prompted, and she frowned up at him, wondering why he needed to ask.

'Do you think he'd want me to know?' she asked. 'He already thinks I take far too much interest in your family affairs, and he'd be sure to think I deliberately went out of my way to see into that end room.' Looking up at him she frowned anxiously. 'Oh, Vincenzo, you know he'd rather I'd been with you this morning than in that room. I daren't tell him, I—I didn't want to.'

'Because you are afraid of him?'

He asked as if the prospect intrigued him rather, and she shook her head firmly. 'Because I'd hate to—to hurt or embarrass him. And you know how he'd feel if he discovered I'd not only seen her but spoken to her and knew who she was.'

Vincenzo kept his arm around her waist, and Helen felt the strong pressure of his fingers in her flesh as they approached the house, saw the oddly closed expression on his face and the way his eyes seemed to avoid looking at her. 'But you do not mind to say this to me?' he asked.

'Why—no.' She was still frowning, puzzled by something in his manner that she did not begin to understand. 'I'm sorry, Vincenzo, perhaps I shouldn't have said anything to you either, it isn't my business, as Guido would be the first to point out. It was just that——' She groped for words, wondering if she even knew the reason herself. 'I needed to tell someone.'

'So?'

That reminded her so much of Guido that she hastily shook her head. 'The woman—Teresa Pucelli, she called her Signora Alessio. Vincenzo, *is* she Guido's wife?'

He stopped at the foot of the steps up to the front door and looked at her for a second, then he laughed; a harsh, wild laugh that prickled her scalp as she stared at him. Then he curled his arm more tightly around her and bent to kiss her mouth, his free hand stroking the silky pale hair back from her face before twining his fingers into it.

When he raised his head again his eyes gleamed darkly and his full lower lip curled, faintly derisive, when he smiled. 'Oh, my Helen, how involved you have become, eh? Let us say that she is our—skeleton in the cupboard, yes?' He kissed her again, so forcefully that Helen tried to turn away, her hands pushing against him. 'And do not think to keep your secret from Guido, *cara mia*,' he added with a glint of malice. 'Teresa will tell him, you may be sure of it!'

Vincenzo was right about Teresa Pucelli telling Guido about her visit, and she must have done so the same day. For when Helen was on her way downstairs to dinner that evening he came along behind her, catching up with her when she was halfway down the stairs and touching her arm as if to draw her attention to him. As if she could remain unaware of him, for she had hastily to subdue the wild urgency of her pulse when his fingers pressed lightly into her flesh.

He was dressed in a formal suit, as he always was for the evening meal, and the light grey with a pale blue shirt was stunningly effective in contrast to his darkness. He never failed to have an effect on her, and try as she would, Helen could not still the clamour of her senses at his nearness. He always seemed so much taller close to as well, especially when she was wearing lower heels than usual, and he seemed to tower over her, bringing a suggestion of menace, with his black eyes and lithe, catlike walk.

'We will walk for a few moments in the garden,' he said, without even attempting to disguise it as a request, and added quickly when she would have said something, 'There is time enough before dinner.'

Determined to have her say, Helen glanced at the *salotto* door. She knew Vincenzo would be waiting there for her to join the rest of the family, and she had said she would be no more than a few minutes. 'I promised Vincenzo——'

'Vincenzo will have the rest of the evening in which to pay you compliments,' Guido interrupted shortly, and when they arrived in the hall he guided her firmly and inexorably towards the rear door into the gardens. 'For the moment I wish to speak with you, Helen, and I have no intention of being put off, nor will you walk away from me as you did this morning.'

In this present mood it would be useless to try and put him off, Helen thought ruefully, and obediently preceded him through the door into the garden. The evening air was quite chill and her dress had only tiny sleeves, so that she shivered as she stepped into the October twilight garden. 'I'm cold,' she began, then caught her breath when he placed a firm warm arm around her shoulders, drawing her to the warmth of his body.

Catching her reaction, he looked down at her and just for a moment she thought a hint of a smile hovered at the corner of his mouth. 'I am sure that Vincenzo has often kept you warm in the same way,' he said, and Helen made no attempt to deny it.

She said nothing, but walked with him along the shadowy path. The garden seemed curiously still and secretive in the autumn evening light, and there were few flowers left now, only heavy-headed late roses and aromatic shrubs to scent the air. The beginnings of a light wind stirred the sprawling cloud and the sun was almost spent, sliding languidly behind the landscape of olive trees and cypresses.

Helen would have been content to do no more than walk, held in the warm circle of his arm, but for the very subject he had brought her out there to discuss. She had no doubt that he had spoken with Teresa Pucelli, and her stomach crawled with the anxiety of anticipation while she waited for what seemed like an interminable while for him to come to the point. In the end she could bear it no longer, and it was she who eventually broke the silence.

'I can guess you've seen Teresa Pucelli,' she said, sounding faintly defiant, 'You knew that I'd been into the room at the end of the gallery when you saw me this morning.'

'I know,' Guido confirmed with unexpected temperance. 'What I do not know, and wish to find out, is how you came to be there.'

Too uncertain of him to plunge headlong, Helen took her time. There was a kind of reassurance in that arm encircling her shoulders and it helped, but she did not take its comfort too much at face value. 'Didn't she —Teresa Pucelli tell you?' she asked, and a glimpse of his eyes when they turned on her was enough. 'I saw— someone coming from my bedroom and realised she was my midnight visitor. I recognised her.'

'So easily?' He seemed to doubt it, but Helen nodded firmly.

'The figure, the long dress and—I don't know, something about her. I knew it was the same woman I'd seen that night, I was certain of it.'

'And you were curious!'

It was a statement, not a question, and Helen noticed the tone of his voice and flushed. 'Yes, I was curious,' she admitted, 'but that wasn't why I was in her room, Guido; I hadn't much option. She seemed to be trying to ask me about something, I think she was asking who I was, but apparently she didn't speak English and I don't speak enough Italian to understand her. She was so agitated and I didn't know what to do for the best.' She hesitated, remembering again those huge and alarmingly blank eyes, and shrinking from the memory. 'I thought it was best to persuade her to go back to her room if I could, she looked so—ill.'

He knew well enough what she meant, and there was a depth of sorrow in his voice that aroused her pity to a dangerous degree. 'She would not have hurt you, Helen. There was no danger.'

What could she say? How could she tell him what she felt, how she pitied him? Guido Alessio was not a man to accept pity readily. Her hands held tightly together Helen tried to find words; to find something to say that would sound neither too trite nor yet unfeeling, but she could find nothing but the obvious.

'I'm sorry, Guido.'

The words came out almost without conscious effort on her part, and Helen caught the swift turn of his head, felt the black eyes raking over her flushed face. It appeared quite incidental when his arm was removed from her shoulders and he turned to face the house once more, but Helen felt the sudden chill that made her shiver, more than the exposure of her flimsily clad shoulders to the evening cool.

Then he turned back to her as she came up beside him and took her once more into the curve of his arm as they walked slowly back to the house. But there was more, Helen's senses told her so, though she had no idea what it was that sat so heavily on his mind. Not until they were in sight of the door did he drop the first hint.

'Have you seen the necklace—the Tears of Venus,

again since that night, Helen?'

Breathing seemed more difficult suddenly and she gazed up at him in the uncertain light with wide eyes, trying to read something into that unfathomable expression, and failing as she most often did. 'How could I?' she asked, steadying her voice. 'Your—Signora Alessio wasn't wearing it this morning, and I've never seen her apart from those two occasions you know about.' Heavy black lashes made darker shadows on his bronzed cheeks, and she did not like it when Guido was evasive. It disturbed her without her being quite sure why it should. 'What is it about that necklace?' she asked. 'You made quite an issue of it the night of the festival, and now you're asking me again. As if you didn't know——' She stopped and her heart was thudding hard, so hard she could scarcely breathe. 'Guido? The Tears of Venus—what's happened to it?'

He stood silently immobile for a moment while Helen looked up at him, willing him to let down the barrier he so determinedly put up between them. Then he reached past her and opened the door into the house, a hand under her arm persuading her inside. Following close on her heels, he kept a fingertip touch on her until she turned and faced him in the brightly-lit hall.

'Guido?'

It was an irresistible plea and after a second or two he shook his head as if to clear it, brushing one hand through the thick hair over his brow. 'It need not concern you, Helen,' he began, but in this instance she was not going to let him get away with that.

'It *does* concern me,' she insisted in a small husky voice. 'You've made it my concern, Guido, and I must know why you're so interested in whether or not I've seen the Tears of Venus again.'

He looked directly at her suddenly and she tried to see something in his eyes that would give her a clue. 'It is missing,' he said quietly, and she caught her breath. 'It has been missing for several weeks.'

'Since that night,' Helen guessed in a whisper, and shook her head slowly while his meaning sank in. How could she help remembering that evening in his office when he had become so angry because she suggested he might one day accuse her of theft? 'And you think that I——'

The pressure of his fingers on her arm silenced her and set her pulse racing, but in the same moment that he looked about to reply, the *salotto* door was flung wide and Vincenzo appeared. He hesitated briefly when he saw them there and recognised that he had very obviously chosen a bad moment to join them, then he slammed the *salotto* door shut and came hurrying across.

His eyes glittered darkly and he flung a firm and very possessive arm about Helen's shoulders while giving his brother a long, narrow look that glittered with suspicion. 'I was under the impression,' he said to Helen very pedantically, 'that you were to join me as soon as you came downstairs, but it seems you forgot, *mia carina*, did you not?'

Helen half turned towards Guido, but completely ignoring him, Vincenzo turned her roughly into his arms and kissed her. A kiss that had neither gentleness nor affection, but only the raw, angry passion of jealousy. Knowing Guido was there made Helen fight him furiously, and the harder she struggled, the more determined Vincenzo was to go on kissing her. It was only when he let her go at last that she realised Guido was gone, and the *salotto* door closed behind him.

'Was that necessary?' she demanded of Vincenzo, and he looked at her and frowned, his arm still possessively encircling her shoulders.

'To remind you that it was me you promised to see before dinner, not Guido?' he asked. 'It seemed so,

Helen! That little scene I saw when I opened the *salotto* door looked just a little too—intimate for my taste!'

'Oh, what nonsense you talk!' She shrugged off his arm, but made no attempt to join the rest of the family in the *salotto* for the moment, she was still too troubled by what Guido had told her about the Tears of Venus. 'What Guido had to say to me wasn't anything at all like you seem to suspect,' she told him, and looked up at him with the anxiety she felt still plain in her eyes. 'Vincenzo, he believes—Guido thinks I know something about——'

He silenced her swiftly with another brief hard kiss and his dark eyes gleamed with a curiously disturbing brightness. 'As long as he was not——' He shrugged expressive shoulders and conveyed his meaning so explicitly that Helen almost blushed. 'We are waiting dinner, *carissima*, so let us go.' He curved one long slim hand about her chin and lifted her face to him. 'And do not mind what Guido says or thinks—it does not matter!'

But it was a precept Helen could not go along with, though she did not say so to Vincenzo. It mattered very much to her what Guido said and thought, but for the moment there was nothing more she could do about it.

CHAPTER SIX

ISABELLA had fully recovered her normal sunny manner the following morning, just as Helen anticipated. Not only was she naturally of a happy disposition, but she had the excitement of a new cousin to anticipate, for there was the prospect of Bianca's baby being born very soon now, and rather earlier than expected. She had no cousins, she told Helen, and she looked forward to the little boy that her Uncle Pietro had promised her.

Less convinced of the infallibility of the expectant father, Helen nevertheless had not the heart to disillusion her, and she shared the general excitement at the coming event. In fact Helen now knew the reason for Pietro's almost frantic concern for his wife, for she had learned that in eight years of marriage Bianca had miscarried several times, and that they pinned all their hopes on this baby being born safely. At the moment the Alessio family future seemed to depend entirely upon Isabella, and there was little sign at present of either Vincenzo or Guido doing anything to remedy the situation.

Although she could not fully comprehend the anxiety of her elders, Isabella was bound to be affected by the air of anxious excitement, and she found it very hard to concentrate on lessons. The talk at lunch time had been of little else but the coming baby, for that morning Bianca had been detained in hospital after her regular check-up. Her time was imminent and no chances must be taken.

With Pietro so concerned with his wife, a great deal of his work was undertaken by Vincenzo. He did it readily enough, but it left him very little time for long lunch hours and consequently Helen found herself with time on her hands. Time which she decided could be well spent doing various small jobs in her room until the afternoon session in the schoolroom began.

In fact she had a great deal on her mind. Last night she had tried to get Vincenzo to enlighten her about the fate of the Tears of Venus, but he had shrugged the matter off, preferring not to talk about it, so he told her. In fact it crossed her mind when he had gone hurrying back to work immediately after his midday meal that he might have done so in part to avoid further curiosity on her part.

Standing at the window in her bedroom, she gazed down into the garden and beyond, to the slightly hazy hillside and soft autumn sky, to Santa Caterina nestling in the hollow of the hills and reminding her of what she still thought of as the happiest few hours of her life. No man had ever made such an impact on her life as Guido Alessio had done, and she had been thinking quite a lot since last night, about the wisdom of staying on in too close proximity to Guido and the temptation he presented.

The thought came into her mind again as she gazed at the hazy autumn countryside below her, and she shrugged uneasily, glancing at her wristwatch as she did so. It was almost time to go in search of her pupil, and she sighed at her own unwillingness to come to a decision. Reaching absently for a bottle of perfume on the dressing-table she took out the stopper and dabbed it on her wrists and neck while she still gazed out of the window.

The perfume was in a big extravagant flagon with an enormous cut glass stopper, one that Vincenzo had given her. She was not over-fond of the scent, but she used it occasionally just to please him, careful not to use it too generously. Still sunk in her own musings, she attempted to replace the top without looking what she was doing and, not surprisingly, fumbled clumsily, then dropped it, murmuring crossly to herself when it shot out of sight beneath the wardrobe.

Whether she liked it or not, the perfume was expensive and without its stopper it would evaporate, so she was obliged to go down on hands and knees to retrieve it. There was a gap of some two or three inches under the massive wardrobe, so she should be able to reach it easily enough.

It was doubtful if the wardrobe was moved very often even for cleaning, for it would take two or three strong men to move it, and the furring of grey dust under there was only what she expected. The glass stopper was easily reached, being lodged just under the edge, but what set her heart thudding hard and made her sit back on her heels with her hands to her mouth was a glimpse she had of something else under there. Something that glittered and gleamed even in the dust-laden darkness under the wardrobe.

It was several moments before she dared look again, and she completely forgot about Isabella and the afternoon schedule as she knelt there trying to gather her wits. She had little doubt that what she had seen was the Tears of Venus, but what she could not for the moment think of was how it got there, nor was she quite sure how she was going to get at it, since it was well back and looked to be out of reach. Acting purely by instinct, she replaced the stopper in the bottle of perfume before going down on her knees again, bending so far down that her cheek rested on the carpet, and squinting one eye along the dusty floor to the bright winking lure of the gems.

She tried pushing an arm underneath, but the floor of the wardrobe was so low that even her slim arm would not reach, and she looked around for something to extend her reach. A comb offered a solution and she crouched down yet again, breathing hard as she poked at the mocking glitter so elusively tucked away. Then she stretched just that little bit farther and gave an audible sigh of satisfaction when at last she felt the unyielding stones, and slowly and carefully, almost holding her breath, she drew the necklace out into the daylight.

Tufts of grey fluff adhered to it but did nothing to dim the fire of the tear-shaped gems that hung from a string of smaller but no less perfect stones, tiny, elusive rainbows darting with every slight movement. For several moments she knelt there looking at it suspended from one shaking hand, overawed by the sheer richness of it and too dazzled to try and think how she was going to explain its being in her possession.

A sudden light tap on her bedroom door brought a choking urgency to her heartbeat and she turned her head swiftly and stared, without moving, until another, more impatient, tap brought her quickly to her feet. She should have answered, she realised it in the moment when the door began to open and a familiar, unfriendly voice demanded her attention.

'*Signorina*, are you not aware that it is——'

Olivia Alessio stopped and her hand on the door handle tightened perceptibly. Her dark, sharp eyes were fixed unwaveringly on the necklace that still dangled in full view from Helen's trembling hand, but she said nothing for several moments, and Helen was too startled, too alarmed to speak. She could only stare at her and try to cope with the urgent clamour of her pulse, for the one person guaranteed to put the worst possible construction on the present situation was this darkly disapproving aunt of Guido's.

'So,' Signorina Alessio said softly, 'we have solved the mystery, eh, Signorina Purvis?' Her tall thin figure was drawn up to its full autocratic height and there was a cruel tightness about her mouth that suggested she might even be enjoying the situation. 'You will come with me,' she said in her strongly accented English, 'and we will see what my nephew has to say about *this*!'

Jarred into action at last, Helen shook her head and grasped the necklace so tightly in her hand that the hard stones cut into her palm, wishing fervently that she had never seen the Tears of Venus. 'I found the necklace down there, underneath the wardrobe,' she explained. 'I can't think how it got there, but I saw it when I——'

'Do not attempt to deter me with your explanations,' Olivia Alessio told her sharply, 'my nephew will deal with you, I will see to it that he does! It is his duty to call in *la polizia*, and this will be sufficient to convince him of the kind of woman he harbours beneath our roof!'

The remembrance of that night when Guido came into her room stayed firmly in Helen's mind, and she knew without doubt that it was that incident that was behind Olivia Alessio's present malice. Helen had heard her that night after Guido left her to go to Isabella, and she could imagine what her opinion had been then; it had probably rankled with her ever since that Guido had somehow gained her promise of silence.

'You're quite wrong, *signorina*,' Helen began, but an imperious hand silenced her firmly.

'I have seen you with my own eyes, holding the necklace in your hand,' Signorina Alessio reminded her, and the eyes she mentioned glowed darkly with evident satisfaction. 'You may believe that because my nephew came to you in the middle of the night you are immune, *mia ragazza*, but you will find him less kindly when he discovers that you are a thief as well as a *civetta*!'

It took no great effort to guess the name she was being called, and Helen flushed. 'Signorina Alessio——'

'*Venga!*' her accuser ordered sharply, and stood back,

one hand on the door handle still, her face as hard and unyielding as the diamonds that pressed painfully into Helen's palm, and Helen had little choice but to obey. '*Si sbrighi!*'

Helen's one hope was that Guido would be less hasty and relentless in his judgment than his aunt anticipated, but she found herself shaking like a leaf as she walked along the gallery and down the stairs. He must surely believe she had known nothing about the necklace until she found it only a matter of minutes ago, and yet it had been only last evening that he told her about it being missing. The coincidence was almost too damning, and she had accused him of suspecting her, a suggestion he had never actually denied. She was very close to tears as she crossed the hall to his office with Olivia Alessio in stern attendance, though she clung grimly to her self-control.

'*Avanti!*'

She thought he sounded more surprised than annoyed at being interrupted, and took what comfort she could from that. Signorina Alessio opened the door wide and swept Helen in before her, then closed it firmly behind them, facing her nephew with her narrowed eyes gleaming. When Helen stopped short just inside the door, she prodded her forward like a beast to the slaughter, and when Guido got to his feet he was frowning at them both curiously.

'Tia Olivia?' The tone of his voice suggested he was vaguely uneasy, and thus prompted, Signorina Alessio needed no second bidding. She launched into a spate of Italian, and stopped very unwillingly when he raised a hand. 'In English, Tia Olivia, *per piacere*!'

The glance he gave her was sufficient to convince Helen that enough had been said already in Italian for him to have some idea of why they were there, and she wished he had not looked away again so quickly. With equal relish but less fluency Olivia Alessio repeated her accusation with passionate harshness; in too rapid English that became almost unintelligible.

'You need wonder no more what has become of *il Pianto della Venus*! This woman has it in her hands, I caught her with it before it could be hidden again! And you would have me silent to protect the reputation of such as her! Hah! *Guardi!*' She gripped Helen's wrist and pulled open her unresisting fingers, exposing the glittering beauty of the gems lying in a palm impressed with sharp red marks. 'You see!'

Helen was close to tears and she watched Guido's face anxiously, saw the expressions that flitted across the strong imperious features betraying everything from initial shock to complete bafflement. But the moment the black eyes were raised and met hers she shook her head and touched a moistening tongue to her lips.

'I found it in my room,' she told him, keeping her voice as steady as she was able in the circumstances. 'I was going to bring it to you, Guido, but Signorina Alessio came in and——'

'Into your bedroom?'

He looked sharply at his aunt and the older woman lifted her chin, haughty in her own defence. 'The *signorina* was late returning to the schoolroom,' she explained, 'and I was passing her door so that I reminded her of the time. When she did not reply to my knock I opened the door and saw her with *il Pianto della Venus* in her hand. It was enough,' she added grimly, and Helen shook her head.

'Helen?'

Inevitably her stunned senses responded to his stern enquiry, and she looked at him standing the other side of the desk. It was always so hard to know what Guido was thinking, but she thought he would surely be more passionately angry by now if he believed his aunt's story without reservation.

'What Signorina Alessio says is true to a point,' she told him in a shakily husky voice, 'but I was telling the truth as well. I *was* late going back to Isabella, but I wouldn't have been quite so late if I hadn't dropped the stopper off a bottle of perfume. It rolled underneath the wardrobe and when I got down on my hands and knees to get it I saw the necklace.'

'Beneath the wardrobe in your room?'

The thread of doubt in his voice made her heart hammer even more urgently, but she nodded her head. 'It's a huge thing and I doubt if it's moved very often, so heaven knows how long the necklace has been there; I wouldn't have seen it then if I hadn't dropped the top off the perfume bottle. I'd just managed to retrieve it when Signorina Alessio came in.' She glanced at her accuser's dark flushed face and noticed the lips curl in disbelief. 'I suppose it did look bad when I didn't answer, but I was too—too stunned for a moment to realise there was anyone there.'

It wasn't easy, but she looked across at Guido and held his gaze until the black eyes seemed to bore into her, and she had never wished more fervently than now that she could tell what was going on behind them. Her heart refused to accept that he could condemn her as a thief on the word of the vindictive woman who frowned at him so impatiently, waiting for him to take the action she expected.

'You will call in *la polizia*!' Olivia Alessio insisted. 'Guido, *chiame la polizia*!'

It seemed such an interminable time before he replied, and Helen felt the warm flood of relief flow through her when she realised he was shaking his head. 'I think not, Tia,' he said. 'It is sufficient that it has been found and returned.' He added something in their own tongue for his aunt's benefit, although clearly Signorina Alessio was far from happy to let it end there. Her sharp eyes glittered dislike, but even so she eventually inclined her head in assent, her reason for doing so becoming clear the moment she spoke. 'I agree, there is no good can come from involving *la polizia*,' she said in her harsh, flat voice. 'The Alessio have never been touched by scandal, and your—involvement, as well as Vincenzo's, with this woman would ensure too much unpalatable publicity. *Cosi!* There is an end of the matter!'

Flushed and far from as satisfied as she was evidently expected to be, Helen looked from one to the other. Her legs felt almost too shaky to support her and she brushed a strand of hair back from her forehead, summoning all her dwindling confidence. 'Not quite!' she said in a shakily insistent voice. 'I've been accused of stealing, a fact that so far no one's taken into consideration. I'm *not* a thief and I want that settled once and for all before anyone leaves this room!' She left no doubt as to who she blamed most. 'Signorina Alessio?'

Olivia Alessio frowned, but it was difficult to guess just what prompted her reply; possibly the dislike she professed of having the matter made public. Whatever the reason she inclined her head after a moment or two, fixing her sharp dark eyes on Helen. 'I am for the moment prepared to submit to my nephew's decision,' she said. 'Whether or not he is proved to be wrong is something no one can forecast! Now—with or without your permission, *signorina*, I shall go to my own room and leave your employer to deal with you as he sees fit!'

No one, not even Guido, Helen thought dazedly, would have dared to try and stop her after that parting shot, and Olivia Alessio walked stiff-backed to the door, closing it firmly behind her. Being alone with Guido was a situation Helen would have avoided if she could, but one thing struck her quite unmistakably as she turned to face him again. He had not, in fact, declared her innocent of theft, but had simply made the most convenient decision for his family pride, and when she looked at him her chin was set at an angle and her eyes bright and wary between their thick lashes.

'You haven't said you believe me, have you?' she asked throatily. 'You simply want to let the matter drop to save a scandal. You think you're letting me get away with stealing your precious family heirloom and being very—magnanimous! Well, you——'

'That will do!'

He stopped her firmly, and she realised that reaction had brought her to the brink of hysteria. Tears stood in her eyes and her hands were tightly clenched, her whole body shaking as she looked at him, and for a moment she felt a searing hatred for the gleaming circlet of gems that now lay on his desk.

'You didn't argue with your aunt when she called me a thief,' she accused in a shiveringly unsteady voice. 'You didn't even try to see it from my point of view.'

He stood on the far side of the desk from her still and the black eyes regarded her steadily. 'I have not accused you of taking it, Helen, you cannot say that.'

'But you didn't deny it!' Helen insisted shakily. 'You simply—you——' Tears brimmed in her eyes and she could hardly see his face for them, but she felt the need to berate somebody and his opinion seemed to matter so much more than his aunt's did. 'Oh, you're so—so devious, I never know what you're thinking! I simply don't understand you!'

She caught her breath and stepped back instinctively when he came round the desk and took her hands in his, his strong fingers squeezing hard. 'Helen, that is enough!'

'And stop speaking to me as you do to Isabella, I resent it!'

'*Madre di Dio!*' Guido swore. 'Will you stop making a martyr of yourself?'

He was too close and her body responded to him as it always did, but now there was the thought of his tragically lovely Violante between them, and she went on rashly, using anger to subdue other more urgent and dangerous emotions. 'You have the necklace back and since you've decided not to have me locked up for stealing it, I'd like to go back to my job, if you don't mind. That is,' she added bitterly, 'if you haven't decided to sack me in case I prove a bad influence on your daughter! Your aunt said she'd leave you to deal with me, and I imagine she expects something of the sort!'

Guido murmured something in Italian and in the same moment reached out for her before she realised his intent, pulling her into his arms, his mouth buried deep in hers and stifling not only the words she berated him with, but her breath too. It was a fierce, hard kiss, and brooked no resistance, not that Helen thought of resisting, for every nerve in her body clamoured wildly in response and her mouth yielded softly to the assault.

When he released her she felt herself on the brink of oblivion, and she stayed close in his arms until she recovered her breath. Looking up, she found the black eyes on her, deep and gleaming, and a curiously bitter smile on his lips. 'I have always found that a very effective way of silencing a woman,' he observed. 'Especially when she is talking nonsense!'

Shaken and not thinking very clearly, Helen shook her head. She reached behind her and broke his hold, then stepped back quickly, not daring to look at him again because it was much easier than she had thought to forget he had a wife. She brushed down her dress and put a hand to her hair, thankful to notice that it did not show how much it was trembling.

'May I go now?' she asked in a small cool voice that must give quite the wrong impression of the way she felt.

She thought he frowned briefly, as if her response was not what he expected. He did not give his consent to her going, nor did he refuse it, but merely moved back and sat on the edge of his desk, reaching for one of the wickedly strong cigars he smoked. 'If I had been convinced that the necklace was stolen I should not have waited all this time before doing something about it,' he said, and Helen's head jerked up swiftly, her eyes wide and puzzled. 'My stepmother is in the habit of mislaying it, and in this instance I imagine it was dropped that night you saw her in your room and, without anyone noticing the fact, it was kicked underneath your wardrobe, where you found it.'

Helen stared at him. 'Then—then you *do* believe me?'

'I have never said I did not,' Guido reminded her. 'The accusations were all on your side.'

Getting up from the edge of the desk he stood for a moment, tall and imperious, his autocratic features half concealed by the pungent, drifting smoke, while Helen watched him dazedly. Then he inclined his head briefly and walked around to the other side, sprawling lazily in the big leather armchair while he regarded her through short thick lashes, that sensual lower lip thrust out temptingly.

'Now you may go, if you wish, and get on with your work, I shall not trouble you again, you may rest assured!'

Oh, how he resented her cool response to his kiss, Helen thought dazedly, and licked her lips anxiously as she turned to go. It had not even occurred to her that someone like Violante Alessio would quite likely mislay her belongings, but Olivia Alessio must have known it, and in the light of that, her action seemed more malicious than ever. Feeling bereft of explanations, she murmured something and left, closing the door quietly behind her. She was more than halfway across the hall before she realised that another section of the jigsaw puzzle had dropped into place without her even noticing, and she spun round quickly, staring at the door of Guido's office.

She could not have been mistaken. Quite clearly Guido had referred to Violante Alessio as his step-mother, and she had been so dazed she had not re-gistered the fact. Her heart was thudding hard at her ribs, and she was almost ready to run back and ask him to confirm it, only after the way she had so coolly requested his permission to return to the schoolroom, she could hardly do that without revealing far too much.

For several minutes she stood there in the wide empty hall and listened to her own wild heartbeat, then she smiled suddenly, and put her clasped hands to her mouth, her eyes bright and gleaming. If the lovely vague-eyed Violante was Guido's stepmother—— She shook her head quickly, not wanting to think be-yond that point for the moment. But she ran the rest of the way to the schoolroom, and she was smiling as she opened the door and went in, her recent ordeal diminished if not forgotten.

Bianca's baby daughter was born two days later, and nothing took precedence over the celebration of her safe delivery, though Helen thought Pietro would have been more delighted still with a son. Isabella was al-lowed to stay up later than usual, and there was cham-pagne for everyone, to drink the new baby's health. It was a mood of celebration that Helen felt able to join in wholeheartedly, although she scarcely realised how often her gaze touched on Guido's face when it warmed with his all too rare smile.

Even Signorina Alessio shared the celebration, whether or not she approved of Pietro's choice of a wife, but her disappointment was if anything more keen than the new father's that the baby was not a boy. It was possibly the champagne that was responsible for some remark she made in Italian when they all sat in the *salotto* shortly after dinner. A remark that Pietro took up in English, so that Helen could appreciate it.

Apparently his aunt had said something to the effect that it was time both Guido and Vincenzo married, and Pietro's bright dark eyes, their glow enhanced by the wine, teased his brothers as he took up the subject with relish. 'Two handsome and virile men unmarried, and the Alessio name in danger of dying out for the want of sons!' he joked. 'Come, *miei fratelli*, will you leave it all to me?'

Helen caught the merest glimpse of Guido's head turned in her direction, but then Vincenzo got up and pulled her to her feet as well and into his arms, smiling at Pietro over the top of her head. 'I am not the marrying kind, Pietro,' he informed his brother, 'so do not look at me to remedy the situation! *Amore*—ah, that is a different matter, but marriage is not for me.' Something his aunt said in Italian made him laugh heartily, and shake his head before he bent and kissed Helen full on her mouth. 'If I married anyone, Tia Olivia, it *would* be Helen, but she knows me better than to expect marriage, eh, *carissima*?'

Hardly knowing where to look, Helen said nothing, but a brief, unwitting glance fell on Guido's face and she noticed a deep dark look in his black eyes that caught at her breath. She was flushing pink with embarrassment at being brought into such a discussion, and she wished especially that Guido need not have witnessed Vincenzo so firmly spelling out his view of her situation.

'You've never mentioned marriage,' she said in a somewhat uncertain voice that she did her best to steady. 'If you had, Vincenzo, I'd have certainly said no.'

Aware that she had stunned him, if not the rest of his family, Helen stood with her eyes downcast and could only guess the way Vincenzo was looking at her. One arm was around her, holding her close to his side, and she felt it tighten imperceptibly, his fingers digging hard into her. 'So?' he asked softly. 'And why not, *bella mia*, eh?' He took her chin in his free hand and tipped up her face to him, dark eyes a little sharper than usual. 'Why would you refuse me?'

'If it is not too difficult for you to believe, Vincenzo,' Guido's voice suggested, 'perhaps it is because she does not love you.'

Vincenzo murmured a quiet oath in his own tongue, then once more laughed aloud. 'Leave such matters to me,' he told him, his smile taunting his brother's seriousness. 'What of you, Guido? You are the head man of our—tribe, *sì*? Why do you not marry and produce the sons that Tia Olivia demands? How does the thought appeal to you, *mio fratello*, eh? Are you not already a success as a *papà*?'

Laughing, he pulled Helen round and with his arm lying heavily across her shoulders they left the warm *salotto* for the cooler air of the garden. He was still laughing as they walked through the chill October evening, lit by a huge yellow moon that cast dancing shadows all along their way. He had probably drunk too much champagne, as they all had, but there was something about Vincenzo's air of wild excitement that made her uneasy.

She wasn't cold, for her dress had long sleeves, but still she shivered, and immediately Vincenzo hugged her closer, nuzzling her neck and murmuring in her ear. Then coming to a halt on the moonlit path, he turned her into his arms and pressed her so close she could scarcely breathe, and he laughed when she put her hands to his chest and tried to loosen his hold on her.

'What is the matter, my Helen?' he whispered, kissing her mouth lingeringly. 'What nonsense Guido talks, eh? Saying that you do not love me; how could that be?' He would find it hard to believe, Helen realised, and wondered why she had never before resented Vincenzo's quite blatant conceit.

'What would you say if I told you he was right?' she asked, and for just a moment he raised his head and stared down at her.

'Ah, no, no, no!' he denied swiftly and confidently, laughing again as he buried his face in the soft paleness of her hair. 'Of course you love me!' His fingers were clumsy, trying to unfasten the neck of her dress and slide it down from her bare shoulder, and his eyes gleamed in the moonlight with a fervour that made her shiver. '*Dio mio, carina mia*, you fill me with such hunger!' His mouth became more searching, his hands more hard and insistent, and Helen found it harder to control the rising sense of panic she felt as she pushed at Vincenzo's chest with her hands, struggling against a strength that threatened to overwhelm her. '*Diletta mia, bella* Elena!'

'Vincenzo, no!' She was free for just a second, but Vincenzo was too quick for her and before she could turn he pulled her back roughly into his arms. 'No, no! I'm going in, let me go!'

Managing to break free again, she ran swiftly before he had time to recover, along the path to the house, followed by Vincenzo's faintly mocking cry. 'Helen! *Mia bella* Elena, come back!'

Ignoring him, Helen hurried on, stopping only when she got to the rear door into the house to put a hand to her hair and press the backs of her fingers to her burning cheeks. Vincenzo must be wondering why she was so adamant about not being kissed, but he had never behaved in quite that way before and she supposed she should have been more discouraging. Also she kept remembering that Violante was not Guido's wife.

She was breathing hard and her face was flushed, her

hair dishevelled despite her efforts to smooth it over, but she was unaware of anyone in the hall until Isabella's voice shrilled out to her, jolting her back to realisation. Apparently Guido thought his daughter had delayed her bedtime for long enough, for he was leading her towards the stairs and the child greeted Helen's sudden appearance as a further excuse to linger.

'Helen!' Isabella called, her voice high with excitement. 'I have had two whole glasses of champagne, have I not, Papà?'

'You have,' Guido agreed, but his eyes were fixed on Helen's flushed face, and her general air of dishevelment, slightly narrowed and darkly speculative. 'But I do not remember you being told you may use such familiarity towards your tutor, *mia ragazza*. What is this, eh?'

He knew why she looked as she did, Helen thought, and wondered if he thought her a party to what had happened, since she had gone willingly enough with his brother. The intensity of that black-eyed scrutiny was well-nigh unbearable, and she hastened to defend Isabella as a means of distracting him from her own position.

'I honestly don't mind being called Helen,' she assured him, but smiled at Isabella as she said it, rather than at him. 'That is if you don't mind, of course.'

He shook his head, obviously thinking of something quite different, and his gaze shifted to the door she had come through. He was so tardy with an answer that Isabella tugged impatiently at his hand. 'Papà!'

'*Sì, sì, mia piccola*.' Isabella frowned at him and clicked her tongue, so that he looked down at her and smiled, one of his rare smiles. 'Of course I do not mind, if Helen does not,' he told her. 'Now will you go to bed with no more fuss, eh?'

Isabella's gaze switched between the two of them, and

she slipped her other hand into Helen's, holding tightly as if she had no intention of letting go. Her object was clear, and Helen was nothing loath to put herself out of Vincenzo's reach for a few minutes. 'You want me to take you up?' she asked, and Isabella nodded, beaming her satisfaction. 'Would you mind?' Helen consulted Guido cautiously, and he looked at her for a moment before he answered, his mind obviously elsewhere.

'Is everything all right, Helen?'

The question took her unawares and she looked startled for a moment, then shook her head, her flushed cheeks taking on even more colour. 'It's nothing I can't handle—thank you,' she said. 'But it might be a good idea to make myself scarce for a while.'

'Ah!' The brief exclamation presumably expressed understanding, and he nodded firmly. 'Then by all means see *la piccola* up to bed.'

'Oh but, Papà, you too!'

Isabella's bright eyes held the mischief of an imp and her tactics were embarrassingly obvious, though Guido showed no sign of resenting them. Nevertheless he made a stipulation that was unlikely to be put aside. 'Very well,' he agreed. 'But you have company as far as your bedroom door only, *mia ragazza*, then Giustina will take over and put you to bed. *Comprendere?*'

'*Sì*, Papà.'

Three abreast they started to mount the stairs, only to be brought up short by the sound of a sharp, harsh bark of laughter from just behind them. Vincenzo stood at the foot of the stairs, arms akimbo, his dark eyes gleaming, but not with amusement, and Helen felt her heart leap with sudden urgency—for no good reason that she could think of, except that something in his eyes made her uneasy.

Even Isabella did not have time to say anything, and Guido's eyes had a watchful, narrowed look. 'So,' said Vincenzo, addressing himself to his brother, 'now you seek to take Helen from me also! Not content with so much, you must take everything, eh? I warn you, *fratello*——'

'Vincenzo!'

Helen heard her own voice faintly and scarcely above a whisper. Vincenzo was drunk, she knew, or he would never have spoken as he had in front of Isabella, for he valued her opinion too highly, and she did not begin to understand the gist of his meaning, apart from his dislike of seeing her with Guido. But that warning made her shiver involuntarily.

Isabella was looking at him uncertainly, held back by some unfamiliar aspect of him that she did not recognise. But she watched him with huge anxious eyes, and after a second or two he opened his arms wide to her. '*Buona notte, bambina,*' he murmured, and immediately Isabella smiled, shaking off Helen and Guido's hands to run back down the couple of steps to where he stood, and throwing her arms around his neck.

'I am sorry, Tio Vincenzo, I did not kiss you good-night!' She remedied the omission enthusiastically, laughing now, though with a hint of that anxious look still lingering in her eyes. '*Buona notte, Tio Vincenzo!*'

He hugged her close, his face hidden for a moment in her long brown hair, then he gazed into her small, pretty face and smiled. '*Buona notte, mia polla,*' he whispered. 'Sleep well.'

Helen was never quite sure what made her look at Guido when she did, but when she glanced at him from the corner of her eye something in his expression made her heart thud hard, for he wore that curiously anxious look again. The look she never understood, as if he feared he might lose his daughter, and that, she had already decided, was ridiculous. It was as if Vincenzo sensed that look too, for he turned his gaze on Guido, and for a moment his eyes were as fathomless as ever his brother's were. Then he smiled again suddenly, though it did not for the moment reach his eyes, and he shrugged, pursing his lips in a suggestion of self-derision.

'I am too high on champagne, *no?*' he said, and the appeal was apparently addressed to his brother. '*Mi dispiace*, Guido.'

'No, no.' Guido forgave him softly and a little wearily, Helen thought, as if he had done so too many times before. Taking his daughter's hand again, he looked down at her, all the warmth of his love for her in his black eyes. 'Come, *piccola*,' he told her, 'it is time you were in bed.' It was quite unexpected, and to Helen quite inexplicable, when he half turned back to Vincenzo. 'Unless you——'

'No, no, no!' Vincenzo's smile had a bright, glittering look to it. 'One *papà* is enough for any *bambina*.' He added something else in Italian and Guido nodded, his strong fingers curling tightly about Isabella's small ones.

'*Grazie*,' he said softly. 'Come, *cara*!'

CHAPTER SEVEN

HELEN was thankful it was Saturday and she could relax for a while. She did not hesitate to accept when Vincenzo suggested they should spend a day in Florence, for it was a trip she had long wanted to make. But the way in which he asked her made it fairly clear that he was not as blandly certain of her acceptance as he would once have been, and she wondered at his having taken her rebuff the other night so much to heart.

Apart from her own part in it, she suspected his recent reticence had something to do with that emotional outburst against Guido, for he had been fractionally less sure of himself ever since then. Obviously Guido had followed his wild and, to Helen, senseless ranting, but she guessed that neither of them was likely to enlighten her as to the reason, so it was useless to speculate.

Driving to Florence through the now familiar hills, she once more found herself wishing there could be some more permanent place for her there. Lately it came all too frequently to mind that one day it was all going to end, just like any other job, and she found it incredibly hard to think of her present situation as just like any other job. She grew daily more reluctant to think of leaving, and knew quite well that it was not simply because of the lovely serene countryside, yet each time another reason thrust itself forward, she resolutely pushed it to the back of her mind, like now.

The vines were gone, and the stripped fields draped naked brown folds over hillsides that had so recently been rich with the grape harvest, while silver-grey olives stood in tortured ranks against a hazily pale sky.

It was autumn and there was a curious sense of sadness in the air, an awareness of spent warmth and vanished fulfilment that Helen found oddly affecting.

It was almost a relief when they drove into Florence, its streets bustlingly busy even this late in the year, and Vincenzo turned to smile at her with a touch of the old familiar boldness in his smile. 'Firenze,' he said, giving the city its Italian name. 'You will love it, Helen, it has everything.'

If that had sounded an extravagant claim, Helen soon discovered how near the truth it was. Although the mass of traffic, the constant chatter of passing motor-bikes and the staggering number of shops were of less interest to her than the ancient buildings and works of art that she had until now only read about, and she meant to enjoy every minute of it.

Vincenzo made only a token objection to her rather daunting programme of things to see, but he warned her that they would need at least a couple of weeks to see even half of it. Even so they managed to cover a lot of ground, mostly on foot, but some of it by car, and he showed her enough palaces and churches to satisfy even the most avid sightseer.

He showed her quiet little *piazzi* and galleries hung with some of the world's greatest art treasures, and the river Arno that cut the city into two, making a reason for building delightful bridges from one side to the other. And when they crossed the Ponte Vecchio, the oldest bridge in Florence, he insisted on buying her a gift from one of the breathtaking displays of gold, silver and jewellery in the shops that were actually part of the bridge. It was a small gold pendant set with a single topaz whose colour, he said, exactly matched her eyes.

Lunch was no more than a brief respite after which he obediently led the way to the Pitti Palace, and from there to the Boboli Gardens where they descended through groves of cypress, oak and pine to more gardens—less colourful than in the height of summer, but quiet and peaceful, and something Helen declared she couldn't miss.

After that they visited the Casa Guido, which she felt was a must if only because it had once been the home of Robert and Elizabeth Browning, and it was already growing dark when Vincenzo eventually called a halt. Drawing her aside from the path of passersby, he leaned against a supporting wall, putting on a face of mock suffering that belied the smile in his eyes.

'Have a heart, Helen!' he pleaded. 'May we not stop for dinner now? I have shown you the whole of Florence in one day and I am dropping with exhaustion and hunger, I swear it!'

Despite her unsympathetic laughter, Helen was feeling much the same way herself, and she was hungry too, she realised, accepting the suggestion unhesitatingly. 'You've got somewhere in mind?' she asked, and Vincenzo nodded, sighing his relief.

'A restaurant, not too far away——'

'And where they know you?' she guessed, her eyes teasing him.

'Of course!' He turned her in the direction of the restaurant and walked with his arm around her waist while he talked. 'We shall dine on the very best food in all Italy, you will see! Mario knows me well and he will see we fare well.' In fact the restaurant was only a few minutes' walk away and when Vincenzo had given the waiter their order he repeated it in detail for Helen's benefit. '*Minestrone casalinga* to begin with.'

'I like *minestrone*,' Helen obliged. 'We have it at home.'

'But not the *minestrone* of Florence,' he insisted. 'It is very special and like nowhere else in the world, especially your poor English broth—ugh!' Ignoring her grimace he went on, rolling his eyes in anticipation. 'Then we will have *bistecca alla Fiorentina*, such big, juicy steaks—mmm! And afterwards——'

'Icecream?' Helen suggested hopefully, for she had a taste for the Italian version, and Vincenzo knew it.

'Icecream,' he agreed. 'You shall have your *gelato, cara mia*, but such as you have never tasted before, special to Florence and Mario's. A *sorbet* flavoured with a liqueur of your choice; how does that appeal to you?'

'It sounds wonderful,' Helen assured him. 'It's been a wonderful day altogether, in fact; thank you, Vincenzo, I don't remember when I enjoyed myself so much. Will you forgive me for tiring you out?'

Vincenzo eyed her thoughtfully for a moment or two, then he leaned forward across the table and stroked her cheek lightly with a forefinger. 'You know, I think I am beginning to like you, lovely Helen,' he said, and laughed when he noticed her puzzled look. 'You do not think it makes sense?' he asked. 'But it does, *cara*, if you think carefully about it. I have loved you and desired you often, but to like—that is different, *no*?'

'I think I know what you mean,' Helen told him, too content at the moment to delve too deeply into profundities, 'but it sounds a little too deep for me at present. I'm too hungry to think about anything else but that steak you promised me!'

He nodded, resting his elbows on the table and reaching with one hand to lift the small gold pendant from her neck, the single topaz glinting warmly in the artificial light. 'But it is because I like you that I wished to give you something like this,' he said. 'You understand?'

'I understand,' Helen assured him. 'And I love it, Vincenzo; I like both the jewel and the sentiment behind it.'

'But *me* you cannot love, eh?'

She felt a curious sense of regret as she looked at him, and shook her head slowly while she tried for the right words. 'I'm sorry, Vincenzo, I almost wish I could even though I know you'd break my heart at the end of it all, as I'm sure you've done a good many others before.' She smiled, taking the malice out of what she felt sure was simply a fact of life. 'You're very good-looking and charming and I like you a lot, but I'm sorry, I'm just not in love with you. But I'll wear the pendant as a—a token, and because it's very pretty.'

'The colour of your eyes,' he reminded her, and continued to study the jewel rather than look at her, his expression more serious than it had been all day. He turned it back and forth for a moment or two to catch the light, then let it go, the warm gold touching her skin with shivering lightness. 'It is not as grand as the Tears of Venus,' he said, 'but it suits you better than that would. You are not hard enough for diamonds, Helen.'

Helen drew a sharp breath and her heart began the familiar rapid fluttering beat as she looked across at him. It was inevitable, of course, that he would have learned about her having been found with the necklace in her possession, sooner or later, and she was unsure whether she would have told him herself or not. As it was she wondered whose version he had heard; Guido's or his aunt's, for it would make a great deal of difference to his impression, she guessed, which of them had told the story.

Surrounded by the warm rich aromas of the restaurant it was easy to account for her heightened colour, but she found it hard to accept his still averted gaze, and her eyes gleamed defensively. True, Vincenzo had made no difference in his behaviour towards her all day, but she firmly believed him less impressed by the more strict moral values of the rest of his family.

'I suppose Signorina Alessio told you that I found the Tears of Venus in my room?' she said, and Vincenzo nodded without speaking. 'Then you'll have gathered that I was caught red-handed by your aunt and hauled up in front of Guido like a thief!'

'Who did not believe you stole it any more than I do,' Vincenzo declared firmly. 'Or any more than Tia Olivia does in her heart.'

Helen smiled ruefully, unable to resist the jibe. 'Has your aunt *got* a heart?' she asked, then almost immediately regretted the words. 'No, I shouldn't say that,' she said. 'I suppose in the circumstances it looked bad for me, and it was inevitable she'd tell you.'

Vincenzo toyed with the fork beside his plate and looked up at her from below arched brows. 'I know you dislike me mentioning it,' he told her, 'but I wished to hear what the circumstances were, Helen, that is my only reason. Tia Olivia gave me only the bare facts.'

'So that you could judge me, too?' she suggested with a hint of bitterness, and he shook his head.

'No, no, I have already told you, I do not believe you took it.'

Helen told him, briefly, what had happened that eventful afternoon, and found herself finding excuses for Olivia Alessio's malicious reaction. 'She probably believed I *had* taken it, in the first shock of seeing me with it,' she allowed. 'And your aunt's never liked the idea of me being Isabella's governess and——'

'My—friend?' Vincenzo suggested softly, one black brow arched wickedly. Then he laughed. 'No, *carissima*, it offends Tia Olivia's sense of propriety to have one of my girl-friends under our roof, and the fact that Guido did not immediately send you home again is another offence to her dignity.'

'So I gathered!'

'It is fortunate that she knows nothing of his kissing you that evening at the *festa*,' he reminded her, and it was clear that he still remembered it and resented it, even though it was over and done with. 'I do not know what she would have said about that!'

Obviously Signorina Alessio had said nothing about Guido coming to her room, and for that Helen was grateful to her, even though her silence was more likely for her nephew's sake than for hers. She traced an invisible pattern on the tablecloth with a finger-end and shook her head, not looking up when she spoke.

'There was nothing there for anyone to make a fuss about,' she said. 'You said yourself that girls get kissed on festival night, Vincenzo, and Guido was only following custom. What's one kiss, after all?'

She said nothing about the other times Guido had kissed her, or come very close to it; like the night she had first seen Violante Alessio. Nor would she have him know what a growing need she had to get closer to his brother, a need that she sought in vain to deny because she was afraid of becoming too deeply involved in something that she knew would hurt unbearably when it ended.

'Of course it was no more than the spirit of the *festa*,' Vincenzo agreed. 'But still I have been surprised by Guido's tolerance where you are concerned; perhaps it is because Isabella is so fond of you. He has always been so strict concerning the people he employs, especially those who have contact with Isabella. I admit I did not expect him to accept you so—so unhesitatingly.'

'And yet you didn't think twice about letting me come here, knowing I might well be sent packing the minute I set foot in the house,' Helen objected. 'You really are selfish, Vincenzo!'

He reached for her hand, squeezing the fingers gently, and his brown eyes were deep and velvety soft as they most often were. 'For all his strictness, my brother is not an unfair man,' he told her, 'and he could not deny that you were every bit as suitable as I had said you were.'

'It was a close thing, just the same,' Helen reminded him quickly. 'He was quite frank about his suspicions that first morning, and he was quite ready to send me back as an undesirable. It was only through Isabella's persistence that I was allowed to stay on.'

'The fact remains that he did *not* send you back,' Vincenzo insisted, 'and that is what Tia Olivia expected him to do when she realised that you and I——' He used expressive hands to convey his meaning. 'You see, Guido has always been—how is it?—the blue-eyed boy? The eldest son and the upholder of the family name and dignity!'

Ignoring the hint of derision, Helen nodded her understanding. 'I can understand that,' she said, 'especially while he was the father of the only grandchild.' She hesitated for a moment before venturing on to what could prove to be very thin ice indeed. 'I know it isn't any of my business, Vincenzo, but you know I've met Signora Alessio; the woman I thought was a ghost when she came in to my room. Violante, I think you called her.'

'You still believe her to be Guido's wife?' he mocked, and Helen shook her head.

'Now I know she isn't,' she told him. 'Guido referred to her as his stepmother.'

'That's right.'

He acknowledged it coolly, but at the same time glanced across the restaurant as if impatient for the waiter to bring their meal. And so bring the conversation to an end, Helen suspected. 'You could have told me that in the first place,' she suggested reproachfully. 'Instead of making such a mystery and letting me think——'

'Does it make so much difference to anything?' Vincenzo interrupted, then smiled with a touch of irony. 'But of course you are curious!'

The same accusing assumption Guido had made, Helen noticed, and frowned. 'Not in the way you imply,' she told him. 'I'm not simply being nosey, Vincenzo, but it could have led to a lot of misunderstanding, my getting the wrong idea.' She didn't tell him that she would have been much less resistant to Guido's kisses that last time if she had known Violante was not his wife, and fortunately he didn't question her meaning.

Resting his elbows on the table, he looked at her reflectively for a moment or two. 'Violante is my mother,' he said, and Helen noticed how much more sober he seemed suddenly. 'Mine and Pietro's. She was only seventeen when she married our father, and he was a widower of thirty-five, but they were very much in love. Guido was already seven years old, so he was only ten years younger than his stepmother, which is perhaps why they got on so well from the beginning. Pietro was born within the year and I came barely a year after that.

'She was never strong, and when my father died five years ago it was too much for her to accept; that was when she became—ill. Tia Olivia was never really happy about my father marrying again, and to someone so young, that is really why she thinks so much more of Guido. She looks upon him as the *real* Alessio, although she is fond of Pietro and me, and of Bianca now that she has the *bambina*.' He smiled at her faintly, a wry and rather touching smile that barely touched his eyes. 'She is not such a monster, our aunt, Helen, but she feels very deeply about the family. To Tia Olivia, Guido is—— He is special. When poor Violante became——'

He spread his hands, unwilling to put words to the reason for those beautiful eyes being so tragically blank, and Helen impulsively reached out to touch him, then drew back. She had never seen that closed, withdrawn look on his face before or felt the air of distance about him, so that she simply clasped her hands together in front of her instead and attempted to ease the conversation into another channel.

'I always thought Guido must be quite a bit older than you and Pietro,' she said, and he nodded, already shedding some of his unfamiliar mood.

'He is ten years older than I am,' he agreed. 'Almost thirty-six now. That is why he is retiring from the show-jumping this year.'

Guido's future plans was a subject of much more interest to Helen than anything else she could think of at the moment, and she ventured a little further with her questions. 'What will he do then?' she asked. 'Join you and Pietro in the family wine business?'

'He is already involved in the business, *cara*,' said Vincenzo, smiling at her ignorance. 'Do you think that riding horses takes all his time? Not so, for he was left the head of the firm when Papà died and he has kept a hand on the reins, in more ways than one for the past five years; he has his office at home, for convenience' sake.'

'I didn't know that. I suppose because I'm so often with Isabella.'

He smiled at her admission, but there was a deep dark gleam of speculation in his eyes as he looked across the restaurant table at her, and he pulled down his lower lip with the thumbs of his clasped hands. 'Would you expect him to confide in you?' he enquired, and Helen, for no good reason that she could think of, flushed a bright pink and hastily looked away. Spotting the waiter coming, Vincenzo greeted his approach with obvious relief and enthusiasm. 'Ah, the *mine-strone*! *Dio mio*, but I am hungry!'

Helen watched him, knowing him thankful to change the subject and leave family affairs alone. Full brothers or not, she mused, the Alessio brothers shared the desire to keep family matters strictly to themselves as far as possible, and she thought Vincenzo had said all he meant to say about his mother and Guido.

They had eaten their meal and were dancing to the seductive strains of a love song before anything of a personal nature was mentioned again. Helen found it hard to be anything other than relaxed and a little dreamy, held close in Vincenzo's arms, and she was content to just drift into a kind of oblivion at the moment, lulled by good food and wine, and music.

'*Romantico*, eh?' Vincenzo's voice intruded into her dream, and he bent to kiss the side of her neck, pressing her close with both arms around her. 'Do you wish it could go on for ever, Helen? You and I and this *umore romantico*?'

If Helen did not reply at once it was because she could more readily accept the eternity of the moment with Guido rather than Vincenzo, but it was a dream she kept to herself, fluttering her eyelashes against Vincenzo's cheek in a kind of assent. It was alarming how often lately she wished herself in Guido's arms again. Not snatched in anger as on the last occasion, but the way it had been at the festival of Saint Catherine before Vincenzo appeared. His arms tight and protective, and his lips so fiercely possessive that she had no choice but to yield to her own wild desires and emotions.

'You are very quiet, *carissima*.' Again Vincenzo's voice snatched her back to reality, and his eyes were looking down at her, soft and velvety dark, warm with desire. 'Are you not happy, *mia bella* Elena?'

Helen banished that disturbing memory from her mind yet again, and smiled. 'Yes, of course I'm happy,' she said. 'I was just thinking, that's all.'

'*Bene!*' He kissed her mouth lightly, almost teasingly, but the look in his eyes shivered a warning along her spine. 'I would hate you to be unhappy,' he whispered. 'Maybe if we wish hard enough it *will* go on for ever, eh, *carissima*?'

'Nothing does, does it?' She had spoken without thinking, voicing her own regret at the inevitable end to her working for Guido, but yet again she thrust the reason for her reluctance firmly out of her mind. Looking up at Vincenzo's curious frown, she offered a quite different explanation. 'Isabella said the other night that she wished I could stay with her for ever and I hadn't the heart to tell her that it wasn't possible; that she won't always be a little girl.'

'How I wish it could be so,' he said. 'Not only that you could stay with us for ever, *cara*, but that Isabella could stay a little girl for ever.'

She pondered on it for a moment, then made a moue of doubt. 'I don't know about that,' she mused. 'Isabella is such a happy soul and she'll probably have a wonderful life; enjoy every minute of it. Why regret her growing up?'

His eyes had the same fathomless mystery that she more usually associated with Guido, but after a moment or two he pursed his lower lip and shrugged. 'Perhaps because she reminds me of my own wild youth,' he said with the air of a man twice his age, and something she glimpsed for only a moment caught at Helen's sympathy without her knowing why. Giving her no time to comment, Vincenzo pulled her more closely into his arms. 'We will dance,' he decreed firmly, 'and talk only of *amore*! No more about the family, I absolutely forbid it!'

He pressed his cheek to hers and moved slowly on in time to the music, and it was a decree that in the circumstances Helen had very little option but to obey. But it did not stop her thinking.

It had been raining when they left the restaurant and it gradually became heavier as they drove out of the city and up into the hills, until it was such a downpour that it was almost impossible to see the road. Vincenzo cursed, frequently and virulently, in his own tongue, and Helen guessed that he was as blinded by the streaming wet as she was herself, even though he knew the road well.

She had never seen it rain so heavily since she came to Italy and it was something she had not anticipated, having seen Tuscany only in its more mellow moods. 'Do you often get downpours like this?' she asked, in part to relieve Vincenzo's obvious tension, and he gave her a very quick glance from the corner of his eye as he leaned towards the windscreen to try and broaden his view.

'Not very often, *grazie a Dio*,' he replied with a trace of grin. 'I cannot see a thing ahead, so it is as well that I know the road, *no?*'

It had got progressively worse and Helen was thanking heaven that they had so far met no other traffic on the narrow hill road, but it was something she expected every second as Vincenzo sent them skimming round yet another corner. 'Do you think we'd better stop for a while?' she ventured. 'It might let up a bit soon, and if you can't see——'

'You are afraid we will finish in someone's vineyard?' he asked, his brief glance faintly mocking. 'Do not concern yourself, Helen, I will not run us off the road, I know it too well!'

The rain was beating on the windscreen, making it a shimmering blur through which it was impossible to see even the bonnet of the car, and Helen felt much less confident than Vincenzo claimed to be. The only sounds were the rattling beat on the windscreen and the roaring shush of water under the wheels, the engine barely audible above it, and the will-o'-the-wisp headlights led them on relentlessly through the downpour.

Helen saw no corner, but by some miracle Vincenzo took them around it, then swore violently when headlights coming from the opposite direction blazed fiercely through the streaming windscreen, turning every drop and rivulet into a blinding prism of light. Wrenching at the wheel, Vincenzo swerved crazily, grappling like a madman with the pull of skidding tires on a greasy wet road, and eventually they brought up nose on to a tree, without actually hitting it.

The engine was dead and the storm now raged unchallenged while Vincenzo dropped his head on to his arms, spread out over the steering wheel. For an awful moment Helen feared he had been hurt, but after only a second or two he raised his head; his arms still flopped over the wheel, he breathed out noisily in relief. His face was pale and he did nothing but stare out of the streaming window for a moment at the trunk of the tree against which the car's radiator rested.

Helen felt sick. Her stomach churned with nausea and her face was chalk-white as she bit very hard on her lower lip to try and stop it quivering. When he turned and looked at her, Vincenzo stared for a moment, then he shook his head slowly and rubbed the back of one wrist across his sweating brow.

'*Madre di Dio*,' he murmured, 'that was too close, Helen.' He reached out and touched her pale cheek, then leaned and kissed her mouth, his fingers stroking soothingly on her face all the time. 'What can I say, *cara*? He was travelling as fast as I was, was it my fault only?'

Unsure whether or not she could find her voice, Helen shook her head, moistening her dry lips with the tip of her tongue. 'Not entirely,' she allowed. 'But that was an ambulance, Vincenzo.'

'So?' He looked surprised. 'I heard nothing, nor did I notice any sign.'

'You were concentrating on the road,' she hastened to assure him, 'but I noticed it in the first few seconds as we came round the corner.' Turning in her seat, she tried to look through the rear window, but could see nothing but rain and darkness. 'I can't see anything, so he must be all right.'

'He almost collected himself two more passengers,' Vincenzo joked grimly, and eyed her for a moment. 'You are sure you are O.K., Helen?' She nodded and he stroked her cheek lightly with a fingertip. 'And you are not afraid to go on with me?'

How could she do anything else? Helen wondered. It was hardly the kind of night to walk home, even had her legs felt capable of carrying her. 'Of course I'm not,' she assured him. 'But take a few minutes' breather first, Vincenzo, you must be shaken as well.'

'I think, *carissima*,' he told her with a touch of grim humour, 'that if I do not drive us home right now, I will not have the nerve to do so at all. So—we go on, O.K.?'

She was shaking and still feeling sick, but she saw little alternative and she nodded. Encouraged, Vincenzo restarted the engine and blew out his breath noisily in relief when it went first time, then backed carefully out on to the road again. The rain was less blinding and she could now see the edge of the road quite easily in the headlights, but still Helen sat near the edge of her seat and the palms of her hands felt clammily moist as they continued on up the narrow hill road. It was as close as she had ever come to serious injury and the experience had left her shaken, she had to admit.

'I wonder who the ambulance was for,' she speculated, trying to ease her own tension, and Vincenzo shrugged.

'Someone else having a *bambino*?' he guessed, and gave her a swift smile. 'Do not take it as an omen, *mia cara*, we are safe enough now, we are almost home.' He reached across and pressed her trembling hands with strong fingers. 'Trust me, will you? Nothing else will happen tonight, you have my word.'

Luckily the Villa Alessio came into sight much sooner than she dared hope, springing up like a mirage when Vincenzo turned the car in through the arched gateway and along the approach. She gave a deep shuddering sigh of relief that she did her best not to let Vincenzo notice, and her tightly clasped hands eased their hold on her handbag when he drew up in front of the door.

'*Là!*' he said, and leaned across to kiss her mouth. 'Did I not promise you we would arrive without any more trouble?' He was half turned in his seat to open the door, when he paused and sniffed loudly, his brows drawn. 'Do you smell burning?' he asked, and Helen shook her head. She was too relieved at the moment to register anything but the fact that they were home safely and without further mishap.

Vincenzo shrugged and got out, coming round to open her door and to lend a welcome hand, for her legs felt alarmingly unsteady when she stepped out into the still pouring rain. Then she too wrinkled her brows and sniffed at the unmistakable stench of smoke in the chill wet atmosphere. Looking at Vincenzo in consternation, she shook her head.

'It *does* smell like burning, Vincenzo; even in this I can smell it.'

For a brief moment their glances met and held uneasily, then both acting on the same irresistible impulse, they ran together up the front steps, and Helen felt his fingers dig hard into her arm when he leaned forward to open the door. The minute she stepped inside Helen stopped dead in her tracks and turned swiftly back to him, her eyes seeking confirmation that she was not dreaming the chaos she walked into.

The smell of smoke was even more overpowering inside the house and it felt chill and damp as it never had before. The blue carpet in its tiled surround was no longer immaculate, but trodden over with muddy footprints, and the vase that normally stood at the foot of the stairs was missing, only a dark patch of spilled water betraying its possible fate.

'*Dio mio!*'

Vincenzo's soft oath muttered against her ear and she clasped his arm with nerveless fingers, looking at him in blank disbelief. 'What on earth can have happened?' she whispered.

Even at a moment like this, she noticed how much older he looked suddenly, and he turned so swiftly that she was almost pulled off her feet when he drew her along with him. She never knew how she walked even that short distance, for her legs were shaking like leaves and her brain was in turmoil, but she went without demur.

They were only half way across the hall when Guido came out of the *salotto* and Helen at once registered the dark severity of his face and the fact that he had a smear of soot across one cheek. His grey suit was crumpled and the front of the jacket torn, his shirt wrenched open as far as his waist and showing a length of sticking plaster taped across the deeply tanned skin.

Seeing it, Helen caught her breath and for a moment her head spun dizzily so that it took all her determination to keep control of her reflexes. Whatever had happened in their absence, Guido had obviously been closely involved, and Vincenzo spoke up quickly, his eyes darting to the stairs.

'Guido, *che c'e*? *Dov'* è Isabella?'

'Isabella is in the *salotto*, she is perfectly all right,' Guido told him, and glanced again at Helen before he went on, speaking slowly and as if he found it hard to believe the words he spoke. It was obvious that for once he would have found it easier to speak in his own tongue, as Vincenzo had, but then Helen would not have understood. 'There was a fire in *l'appartamento*.

Violante was overcome by smoke and both she and Teresa are in hospital.'

'The ambulance we saw,' Helen whispered, and passed her tongue swiftly across dry lips before she explained, 'We almost—we saw an ambulance on our way home. It must have been coming from here.'

'Most likely,' Guido agreed, and turned back to his brother.

'She is not——'

Vincenzo swallowed hard, unable to finish the enquiry, and Guido was shaking his head slowly, making it plain that Violante's condition touched him as deeply as it did her son. 'There is hope for her, Vincenzo,' he told him. 'But the ambulance was late arriving because of the storm, and the delay was—almost too long. We did our best to keep her breathing——'

'Oh, *Dio mio*,' Vincenzo whispered, and put a hand over his mouth, his eyes unashamedly filled with tears suddenly.

Guido took his arm, his strong fingers squeezing courage into Vincenzo's grief, but even now he did not forget Helen; he looked back to make sure that she came with them into the *salotto*. He was a tower of strength, she thought as she followed them dazedly, and wondered just what part he had played in keeping Violante alive until the delayed ambulance arrived.

The sight of Olivia Alessio with red-rimmed eyes was an unexpected one, but Helen felt an uncontrollable sense of pity for the older woman in that moment. She looked so much older and drawn, her piercing black eyes dulled with weeping, and her thin arms wrapped protectively round Isabella, who stood beside her in her nightdress and dressing-gown.

Isabella looked bewildered and more than half asleep, as if she had been woken from a deep slumber and was still not fully aware of what was going on. To Helen the familiarity of the *salotto* was a welcome

comfort and she sank into an armchair gratefully, glad
to relieve her shaking legs of the weight. Guido was
across by the drinks cupboard, she noticed, pouring out
brandy, and she looked up in vague surprise a few
moments later when he held one out to her.

'What has happened?' he asked, and glanced briefly
at Vincenzo sitting some distance away and out of earshot, with his glass of brandy held tightly in tense
fingers. 'You both looked pale and disturbed before you
knew what had happened here. No, no, no,' he added
when she would have replied, 'sip some of your brandy
first.'

He curved his own strong fingers over hers as they
held the brandy goblet, and tilted it towards her, so
that she had little option but to do as he said and drink
some of it. Her hands were shaking and his touch
sparked off other reactions, bringing a warm, comforting glow that had nothing to do with the fiery flow of
brandy into her body.

'What happened to frighten you, Helen?' He allowed the spirit only a few seconds to do its work, then
pressed her for an answer, his black eyes irresistibly
compelling. 'Do not deny there was something,' he
warned, 'I saw it in your eyes and your faces when I
came out.'

'We came through that awful storm,' Helen told
him, 'and we couldn't see a thing; I don't know how
Vincenzo managed to see to drive. We were almost
home when we met an ambulance coming round one
of the bends and we—there was almost a collision.'

Even now her hands felt cold and clammy at the
thought of it, and Guido was frowning. 'So!' he muttered, and his black eyes scanned her face swiftly before switching to his brother.

'We're both O.K.,' Helen assured him quickly.'We
didn't hit anything, not even the tree we fetched up
against when we ran off the road, but we're a bit

shaken. And then to come home to this!'

'You are sure you are not hurt?' he insisted, and she nodded.

'Quite sure, Guido. I doubt if either of us has even a bruise, but it was a near thing, and I'm very glad of this brandy.'

'*Grazie a Dio!*'

Normally she would not have dreamed of questioning him as she did, but nothing about this evening was normal, and she felt a quite genuine concern for the woman she had seen only twice, but felt a very real pity for. 'What happened here, Guido?' she whispered. 'How did the fire start?'

He did not sit down and Helen wished he would, for he seemed too remote while he continued to stand. He did not reply at once, but after a moment or two he shrugged his broad shoulders. 'No one seems to know for certain,' he said. 'Teresa was not with her and she came back to find the apartment full of smoke and Violante in the bedroom, apparently still asleep. She had breathed too much smoke by the time I was able to get to her; we did what we could—but it was so little.'

Her eyes went automatically to the long strip of sticking-plaster across his chest, and she shivered inwardly. 'You—you were hurt,' she whispered, but his reply almost suggested he resented her noticing.

'A scratch only! The bedroom door jammed in the heat and did not open easily.'

It was hard to keep her eyes from the dark breadth of his chest and the column of throat where that oddly vulnerable pulse beat rather more rapidly than normal. She could not have borne it, she told herself, if they had come home to find Guido instead of Violante dangerously ill in hospital, and she shivered once more, quite involuntarily.

'Signora Alessio,' she ventured, and Guido's black

eyes glittered with dark painful truth.

'It is doubtful if she will survive the night.'

She swallowed hard on the poignant frankness of his answer, but said nothing because Isabella had crept up beside him, clinging tightly and seeking the reassurance of his strength. Vincenzo was fun, Helen realised, but Guido was the one she sought at times like this. He looked down at her small tired face and stroked her cheek softly, so that she half closed her eyes, almost falling asleep on her feet.

Bending right down, he kissed her forehead, stroking her hair in a gentle soothing gesture all the while he spoke. 'You must go back to your bed now, *carina*. Shall I take you upstairs?'

Isabella nodded, heavy lids drooping, and Guido swept her up into his arms. Her head was already drooped on to his shoulder when she said goodnight to Helen, and Olivia Alessio got up from her chair and kissed her gently before Guido took her across to where Vincenzo still sat alone, broodingly unhappy and seeking no company but his own at the moment.

'*Buona notte*, Tio Vincenzo.' Her quiet little murmur roused him, and was so different from her customary brightness that he got to his feet quickly and cupped the small face in his hands while he kissed her.

'*Mia dolce bambina*,' he murmured, stroking the light hair back from her face. '*Buona notte*—sleep well, *cara*.' He kissed her again and when he dropped back into his chair there were more tears on his cheeks, Helen noticed.

'There will not be any more smoke, Papà?' Isabella pleaded, her arms wrapped tightly around Guido's neck, and he shook his head firmly.

'No, *mia dolce*, there will be no more smoke, I promise you. You may sleep easily and nothing will hurt you.'

Her eyes were already closed when Guido closed the

salotto door, and as Helen watched them go she felt
again that curious lump in her throat. She could still
not understand her sense of sadness whenever she saw
him with his daughter, but speculated on whether it was
because such tenderness as he showed Isabella was so
unexpected in a character as relentless and autocratic
as his most often was.

It had never struck her before just how much older
he was than her; it must be some thirteen or fourteen
years, and yet she had never felt there was so much difference. Vincenzo had said he was nearly thirty-six, and
that night for the first time she had recognised it in the
severe lines of his face and in the air of maturity about
him when he comforted not only his little daughter,
but Vincenzo and herself too.

They all depended on him so much, it seemed, and
she wondered if even those broad shoulders might not
sometimes grow tired of the burden. Perhaps if there
was someone to—yet again she shook her head over the
now all too familiar fantasy, but found that this time
it was even harder to suppress.

CHAPTER EIGHT

IN daylight the following morning it was more easy to assess the damage done by the fire, but fortunately it had been confined to the flat at the end of the gallery. Although the pungent smell of smoke lingered on in everything from bed-linen to the clothes they wore, and the gallery as well as the hall showed signs of the fire brigade's efforts to keep it contained, there was very little structural damage.

The house felt strangely cold and quiet to Helen as she left her room and looked in on Isabella, and she breathed a sigh of relief to find the small figure still curled up in bed and sleeping soundly. It would do no harm for her to sleep on, and lost schooling could quite easily be caught up another time.

Isabella's smiling and garrulous presence was missed at the breakfast table, though, and it was obvious that the irremovable question in everyone's mind was whether or not Violante Alessio had survived the night. Pietro and Vincenzo both looked so much older than they usually did, and their eyes had a strangely haunted look without their customary smiles, so that it struck Helen how much like their mother they both were. Guido, as usual, had breakfasted early and already gone.

It was difficult to tell what Olivia Alessio was feeling, but this morning Helen took her stern expression less at face value, remembering her red-rimmed eyes last night. Perhaps Vincenzo was right, and their aunt was not the monster she sometimes seemed to be; certainly she had been genuinely affected by her sister in-law's condition last night.

Vincenzo would probably have better kept himself occupied, but instead he went to the hospital, and Pietro was visiting Bianca and the new baby in hospital, so together they waited on the spot for news of Violante. At rather a loose end until Isabella put in an appearance, Helen busied herself in her room rather than stay alone with Signorina Alessio in the *salotto*, but there was only so much she could do and eventually, after having checked again on her charge, she decided to go out. Even though she was not too personally involved, she found the pregnant atmosphere of waiting too overpowering after a while.

The fact that she found herself making for the stable buildings was, Helen told herself, sheer coincidence, but as she made her way round the perimeter of the practice ring her heart was beating much more quickly, and it was quite automatic to glance across for some sign of Guido. He stood in the doorway of the stable, apparently speaking with someone inside, and while he was unaware of her she had the chance to watch him uninhibitedly.

The sun was still shining, but the air was raw and damp after last night's rain, and even that far from the house the stench of smoke still hung heavy and pungent in the atmosphere, reminding her of what had happened. Seeing Guido, she recalled that long strip of plaster strapped across his chest, and his almost terse dismissal of her enquiry. She could still shudder when she considered how easily it could have been him lying in a hospital bed, as Violante was, and her steps instinctively quickened as she walked towards him.

The following week he would be leaving for England, and the competition they had discussed on her last visit to the stables, and she hastily suppressed a sudden urge to ask for leave to go on holiday for a few days in the same week. It would be too obvious; even Isabella would see through it, and Vincenzo would certainly have something to say.

Standing with his hands on his hips he looked quite relaxed, different from last night, and she was suddenly reluctant to do anything to remind him. His feet were slightly apart and his long legs taut and straight; virile and so very masculine, he set her thoughts racing along the now familiar track, and for a moment she did nothing to check them. He wore no jacket, but a thick warm shirt stretched across broad shoulders, open at the neck as always and showing the long column of throat that was the most vulnerable part of him.

One hand held his gloves and hat and the other the long riding cane, and as she approached him, still unobserved, he began tapping the cane against his leg, a now familiar habit that made her smile to herself. Then he realised suddenly and turned towards her so that she could see the unaccustomed dark smudges below his eyes from lack of sleep, and the drawn look that betrayed every one of his thirty-six years.

'Helen?' It was only when he spoke as he did that she realised he anticipated her coming with some kind of message, and she shook her head quickly.

'I just came out for a walk,' she explained, making no excuse for the fact that it sounded like an apology. 'Isabella's still asleep, and I didn't feel like staying in the house.'

He would know what she really meant was that she didn't want to stay alone with his aunt, she guessed, and he was looking at her with the narrowed look that meant he was trying to satisfy himself on some point or other. 'Are you certain you have no ill effects from that near miss that you and Vincenzo had last night?' he asked, and she shook her head.

'Quite sure,' she assured him. 'But what about you? You hurt your chest, it was strapped up last night.'

He turned her about and they walked across to stand by the fence enclosing the practice ring, Guido taking his time about answering her. His shirt was too thick for anything to show through it, and if the strapping was still there it couldn't be seen. 'It is hardly noticeable,' he said, dismissing the subject with the same touch of asperity he had the first time she asked him about it.

But Helen noticed how he rubbed a hand over his chest while he said it, and she suspected it might be troubling him more than he was prepared to admit. 'That's what you told me last night,' she reminded him, surprised by her own bravado. 'But that was an awfully big dressing for a doctor to have put on something you say is hardly noticeable.'

'Blood is very impressive in quantity,' Guido observed dryly. 'Tia Olivia looked as if she was about to faint at the sight of me and I believe Doctor Bennetti put on the dressing as much for her sake as for mine.'

'And you promptly tore it off the moment you had the chance!' Helen guessed. It gave her a thrilling sense of intimacy to be standing with him like this, and her senses responded to him as they always did, whatever had happened or was to happen. 'You did, didn't you, Guido?'

'Are you scolding me?' He spoke softly, and the prospect seemed to be amusing him. Also, she noticed that he leaned towards her a little, and there was a gleaming warmth in his eyes. 'It is nothing, Helen, only a scratch, as I told you.'

'Then I have to believe you, don't I?'

Perhaps it was something in her eyes that challenged him. The wild, urgent beat of her heart must make some outward show, and she was trembling like a leaf when his warmth invaded her skin as he leaned closer. '*Va bene*,' he breathed softly, 'you shall see for yourself whether I am telling the truth or not!'

Helen bit her lip in sudden doubt when without further ado he began to unbutton his shirt, opening it from neck to waist to expose the broad golden chest with its suggestion of black hair. Powerful muscles rippled beneath the skin as he pulled the shirt wide with both hands, and he regarded her with a gleam of challenge.

'*Là!*' he announced, with the air of a man proving his point, and Helen caught her breath.

No doubt it looked worse than it was, but even so the vicious scar sent shivers through her whole body. He had, as she guessed, removed the sticking plaster she had noticed last night, and the marks it had left ran in two long red, sore-looking lines the width of his body, as if he had wrenched it off with his customary impatience. What it had covered was revealed as a mercifully not too deep gash on which the blood had dried like a thick dark cord, and it was that which made her shiver.

'It—it looks awful,' she said, and did not realise how accusing she sounded when she said it. 'You should have left it covered; suppose it goes——'

'Suppose we do not make a fuss about a scratch,' he suggested, but without his usual impatience. He did not for the moment refasten his shirt, but put a hand to the scar as if to ease it. 'It is not serious, Helen, only superficial, it looks much worse than it is.'

Helen found it hard to stand so close and not reach out and soothe the torn flesh with her fingertips. Instead she glanced up and saw his faintly sardonic smile and shook her head. 'It could have been a lot worse,' she agreed, slightly husky-voiced, and her sobriety seemed to remind him of more serious matters as he re-buttoned his shirt.

'Has there been any news from the hospital? No, of course not, or you would have told me! Pietro's gone over again, of course?'

Helen nodded. 'He went over early to see Bianca, and to be on the spot if anything—if there's any news.' They were plunged again into the tragedy of last night, thinking of Violante. 'I'm sure if news comes through someone will come and tell you. Vincenzo's gone with him.'

Helen had never felt quite as she did at that moment, and she did not quite know what to do about it. What she wanted to do was to sympathise about Violante, to comfort him, but she suspected that Guido was not the sort to welcome any display of pity, so she very firmly suppressed the urge. Where they stood they were well out of sight and earshot of the two men working in the stable, so that she gazed at him for much longer and much more intensely than she realised until he turned and looked at her.

'Vincenzo has told you who Violante is, of course?' he said, and Helen nodded, hoping he hadn't noticed her study of him.

'Oh yes, he eventually put me right,' she told him. 'He told me she was his mother—his and Pietro's. He might just as well have been honest about it in the first place!'

'Put you right?' The black eyes encompassed her in their black depth, and Helen realised that she could have phrased it differently. 'What do you mean, Helen —put you right?'

She moistened her lips anxiously, fully aware of that steady black gaze on her, and feeling rather as if she had been trapped. 'I—I just mean that—he confirmed Violante was his mother—your stepmother, as I said.'

'But until then——?' She shook her head, reluctant to tell him her first wild guess. 'Until Vincenzo—put you right, who did you think she was, Helen?' he asked.

It was a moment or two before she had the nerve to tell him, and her heart was pounding hard, her eyes downcast, as she tried to steady her voice and make it sound like a perfectly logical conclusion to have come to. 'I knew she wasn't old enough to be your mother; and the name—I thought—I thought she was your wife.' She made the admission with obvious reluctance, and Guido stared at her incredulously.

'*Buono Dio!*' he breathed. 'What a little fool you are!'

'What else could I think?' Helen demanded, pressing on without thought for the consequences. 'I—I wasn't sure whether or not she was Isabella's mother, but I thought she was your wife.'

'And you believed I was the kind of man who—dallies with young girls while he has a sick wife living under the same roof?' Guido asked in a voice that sent shivers along her spine. '*Dio mio!*'

Helen was trembling so much she was not quite sure how she managed to remain standing, even with the fence to hold on to, and she could not meet his eyes, however hard she tried. Her voice trembled too when she attempted to explain. 'I—I tried to understand,' she whispered. 'It wasn't like you say, I didn't think——'

'You enjoyed my kisses, believing that I was cheating on a wife who was sick in her mind!' Guido charged, as if the very thought of it sickened him. 'And not only that—you thought I might also have an illegitimate daughter, or perhaps more, who knows? Perhaps you imagine I have other Isabellas in various parts of the world, wherever I happen to be competing! Is that what makes you respond so warmly, Helen? The possibility of being ravished by a rake like me? *Dio*, your opinion of me!'

His barely suppressed violence frightened her as she had never been frightened before, and yet she could still allow him reasons for coming to the conclusion he had. But he knew nothing of how long or how often she had fought against falling in love with him, or how often she had avoided being alone with him for fear those few moments at Santa Caterina might be repeated.

There was nothing she could do about the tears that flooded her eyes and rolled down her cheeks, giving her

small face a touchingly childish look. 'I—I didn't know
—not when we went to Santa Caterina; and afterwards,
I tried—I tried not to—I'd seen her and knew what it
must be like, and—and I felt——'

'*Signore! Favorisca venire, signore!*'

The young girl who helped Giustina around the
house came running towards them, panting for breath,
and Guido turned swiftly, giving her his immediate attention, his eyes sharp and his lean body tensed as for
shock. 'Signora Alessio?' he asked tersely, and the girl
nodded.

'*Sì, signore.*' There were traces of tears in the girl's
round brown eyes and obviously she had been affected
by the general atmosphere of grief, if not by personal
shock. '*Mi dispiace, signore,*' she said, and Guido put
an absent hand on her shoulder in recognition of her
sympathy.

'*Grazie,* Renata; *basta.*'

The girl turned and started back, but Guido stood
for a moment as if he needed time to convince himself
of the truth. His violence of a few minutes before was
gone, and he seemed oddly at ease somehow, so that
Helen wondered if, despite the tragedy of Violante's
end, her family might not feel a certain relief that she
would no longer be a sad-eyed prisoner in her luxurious
apartment at the end of the gallery.

When she reached out to touch him it was instinctive, and prompted by her own need, her fingers brushing lightly over the wool shirt sleeve until he looked
at her. 'I'm sorry, Guido,' she whispered.

He merely looked at her for a moment, then a large
hand reached out and brushed down her cheek until it
cupped her chin, the gentle sweep of his thumb taking
away a tear that lingered there. Leaning over her, he
pressed his mouth to hers, and his lips lingered for a
moment afterwards, his breath a warming caress on her
tongue.

'So am I,' he whispered, then turned and followed the girl back to the house.

It went without saying that Guido's trip to England was cancelled, and it was he who arranged everything for his stepmother's last public appearance. He had loved her, Helen never doubted it, although he wept less openly and with less passion than her two sons did. The funeral was an ordeal Helen would willingly have forgone, but it seemed to be expected of her that she would attend, and she had at least been near Guido. Although it was Vincenzo who had clung tightly to her hand throughout the long service. Isabella, mercifully, had been sent to friends.

Once it was over it was amazing how quickly the household seemed to return to normal, and it somehow made it all the more staggering when Vincenzo broke his news to Helen one evening after dinner. Walks in the garden were mostly a thing of the past now, but he had asked that she go with him, and she saw no reason to refuse.

It grew dark much earlier now, of course, but it was surprisingly mild still for the end of October, and it was still pleasant to walk in the garden on a moonlight night. Even though the flowers were all gone, and the air was damp with the threat of further rain, it smelled fresh and clean, and the shrubs and trees sheltered it from the coldest winds, though she wore a coat for all that.

'You know that Guido is coming into the business at the end of this month?' said Vincenzo, breaking into her wandering thoughts. 'Full time, not just part time as he has been until now.'

'I knew he *was* coming in full time, you told me so,' Helen reminded him, 'but I didn't realise it was to be quite so soon.' She looked up, trying to see his face in the pale haze of moonlight. 'That competition in England, the one he missed, was to have been his last, then?'

'It was a pity he missed it, *no*?' Vincenzo suggested with a faintly malicious grin. 'Guido would like to have gone out in a cloud of glory, I am sure.'

'He's won his last four competitions, so I'd say he *did* go out in a cloud of glory,' Helen countered, and speculated yet again on just how envious Vincenzo was of his famous brother. 'Just the same it's a pity he had to miss this last one. He's going to miss his horses and competing in all the big shows.'

'He will miss the competition, but he will still have his horses,' Vincenzo said. 'And he will be too busy at first to even bother with them when he has my work to do as well.'

Obviously Helen was meant to react exactly the way she did, and she frowned up at him curiously. 'I don't get you.'

'You still could, *cara*!' He made the retort with his usual lighthearted bravado, but he was more serious than he appeared, she realised when he brought them to a halt part-way along the garden path. He turned her to face him so that she stood with the moon shining full on her face, turning her light golden hair to silvery white and darkening the smudged shadows of her lashes on her cheeks. 'I shall not be here for very much longer, *mia bella* Elena,' he told her.

It was difficult at first to decide how she felt, but Helen's heart rapped urgently for a few moments as she considered the possibilities. 'Vincenzo—you and Guido—you haven't—I mean, it isn't because he's coming into the business full-time that you're leaving, is it?'

He traced a fingertip round the soft outline of her cheek and shook his head. 'Not for the reasons you perhaps imagine,' he told her. 'I have not quarrelled with Guido and I would willingly work under him, but his coming in has enabled me to free myself. I have decided to venture further afield; I am restless, you see.' He laughed, stroking her hair back from her face. 'Occasionally I am able to travel to England for business reasons,' he enlarged, 'but the company I am to work for in Australia will let me travel all over the world. I am going to sell wine for the Aussies for a change, *cara*; I have decided—it is what I wish to do!'

'Vincenzo!'

It was hard to grasp that he would willingly leave all he had at the Villa Alessio and go to work for strangers, but Vincenzo was, she had to admit, basically a restless spirit and the venture would appeal to him. Though for how long, she would not care to guess. She could not imagine the house without him, either, and when she saw the way he was smiling she felt a surge of affection for him that had nothing to do with romantic love.

'You will miss me, eh?' he asked, though he had no doubt of the answer, she guessed.

'I *shall* miss you,' she admitted unhesitatingly. 'But I don't understand why, Vincenzo. I know you like the idea of travelling the world, but aren't you happy here?'

'But of course I am happy,' he insisted, 'it is simply that I wish to see more places, meet more people.' He rolled his dark eyes wickedly. 'More beautiful girls, eh?' When he saw her mock frown, he laughed and shook his head, mocking her half-hearted disapproval. 'I have told you that I am not the marrying and settling down type of man, have I not? I do believe that with you I could come close to being faithful, as close as I could to any woman, but that is—too uncertain, *no*?' He traced her profile with a light finger, his dark eyes unreadable in the uncertain light. 'You are very much the marrying and settling down type of woman, eh, Helen?'

'You'll miss Isabella,' she said, swiftly evading the

matter of her own feelings. 'And she'll miss you.'

'Ah, *sí*.' His velvet brown eyes softened as they always did whenever Isabella was mentioned. 'I shall miss *mia polla*, but I am not the paternal type of man either. I want no ties, no strings attached, eh?'

'Does Guido know?'

Of course he would know, Helen realised. Vincenzo would not have taken such a step without consulting him, for whatever minor disagreements they might have sometimes, she believed he was more closely attached to Guido than anyone else in the family, except possibly Isabella.

'He is glad to have me go,' Vincenzo told her, but the smile in his eyes gave lie to any suggestion that Guido was glad to see the back of him. Tracing a finger along her jaw, he gazed down at her thoughtfully for a moment, his eyes bright and quizzical. 'You would not come with me even if I had asked you, would you, Helen?'

Knowing he was only half serious enabled her to answer as matter-of-factly as she did. 'No, I'm sorry, Vincenzo, I couldn't.'

'Not unless I made an honest woman of you, eh?' he laughed. 'Oh, I have heard that said,' he told her.

'Not even then,' Helen told him, smiling a little because he was so obviously in high spirits about the venture, however much Violante's death had affected him.

He cocked a black brow at her and again quizzed her response closely. 'Because your interests lie—elsewhere?' he suggested, then exclaimed triumphantly when she coloured. 'Ah-hah!'

'I'm still employed to teach Isabella,' she reminded him defensively. 'Just because you're going off to Australia, Vincenzo, the whole Alessio household isn't going to come to a standstill, you know. Isabella still has to be educated.'

He was evasive suddenly, and Helen could not understand why, frowning at him curiously while he twisted a strand of her pale hair around his fingers. 'Has Guido not told you yet that she is to go to a private day school in Santa Caterina?' he asked, and Helen stared at him.

Her breath seemed caught in her throat and she could feel the urgent thud of her pulse like a drumbeat in her head. 'I—I didn't know,' she stammered, when she could find her voice. 'I had no idea it was even in the air.'

'It is what you have always said should be, is it not?' Vincenzo insisted, and she nodded, unable to argue with him.

What she had not considered, Helen realised, was that with Isabella going to school she would no longer be in need of a governess, and anticipating the inevitable result of that made her feel as if the bottom had suddenly dropped out of her world. 'When?' she ventured, as soon as she could say anything. 'I mean, how long have I got?'

Vincenzo shrugged with what seemed like his customary carelessness, and which in this instance made Helen feel like screaming at him. How could Guido have made such an arrangement without saying a word to her, when he must know she would have to do something about finding another post?

'It is something Guido will explain in his own time,' Vincenzo informed her, and she clenched her hands tightly, wanting to go and find Guido there and then.

'In *my* time too, I hope!' she said, as if there was no more at stake than finding another job. 'Oh, how can he just—*do* things like that, as if no one else matters but him and his plans?'

'Not his plans in this instance,' Vincenzo told her with stunning frankness. 'I told him that I thought it would be good for her. Just as you said it would be.'

'You?' Helen found it hard to believe Guido had allowed himself to be influenced by anyone where Isabella's future was concerned, least of all Vincenzo. Looking up at his face she could tell nothing, except that black lashes hid his eyes and made him look oddly secretive. 'I don't understand why Guido of all people would let you talk him into something like that, Vincenzo. It—it's not like him.'

'No?' He twisted a strand of hair round and round so tightly that she gasped in protest and tried to pull back, but Vincenzo was smiling and he was so obviously very pleased with himself that something trickled along her spine like ice-water and made her shiver suddenly. 'Did he not take you on as her governess on my advice, and has he ever regretted it?'

'Many times, I imagine!' Helen retorted, moving out of his reach. 'He's suspected me enough times of being here for other reasons than teaching her the three R's anyway!'

'Hah!' He dismissed the idea with a wave of his hand, and took her arm as they walked back along the path to the house. 'He knows that you have done your work well, and that Isabella is very fond of you.'

'Then why,' Helen insisted with all her heart in the words, 'is he sending me away? Especially why is he being so—so underhand about it?'

'He is——' Vincenzo squeezed her fingers hard, then leaned and kissed her mouth with his customary lack of inhibition. 'There are many things that Guido has to explain to you,' he told her, 'and I shall not attempt to take on the task in his stead. *Dio mio*,' he added, rolling his eyes frantically, 'he would kill me if I did!'

It struck Helen as ironic that just when she wanted to see Guido and speak with him, she could not manage to get him alone. A number of times in the past he had literally commanded her presence either in his office or elsewhere for the purpose of expounding his opinion of her behaviour, and it seemed a little unfair that now she wished to turn the tables she simply could not manage a suitable time.

She was not only angry about his virtually bringing her job with Isabella to an end without telling her, but hurt because he was apparently ready to dispense with her as he would any other employee whose services he no longer had any use for. She had seen her position as a little more personal than that of any other employee, having been almost treated like one of the family, and the fact that she now frankly admitted to herself that she loved him made the hurt all the more painful.

She had gone to her room much later than usual the night before, in the hope that she might catch him alone when the rest had gone to bed. But even there she was frustrated, for he left the *salotto* with his aunt while Vincenzo was still expounding the virtues of a new and very expensive car he had his eye on. Her best bet seemed to be to get up early and catch him before the rest of the family came down to breakfast, and that she did, the following morning.

She found him in the *salotto*, relaxed and reading the newspapers, and obviously completely unaware of any impending hostility, because he got up from his armchair when she went in and smiled in a way that very nearly undermined her resolve. He wore dark blue slacks and a long-sleeved cream shirt, the latter contrasting with staggering effect with his bronzed face and throat; and he smelled warm and fresh from the shower, so that her senses drank in greedily everything about him.

He looked so completely at ease that she actually felt a twinge of conscience about what she meant to do, but she had steeled herself for it ever since Vincenzo dropped his bombshell the night before, and it had even kept her awake half the night, thinking about it. She was feeling much too emotional, she knew, but it

was something she felt strongly about, and because she
loved him it added despair to the chaos of emotions
that churned away inside her.

'Good morning, Helen, you're very early!'

She did not sit down and consequently he remained
standing, looking at her curiously when she did not
smile but merely murmured a brief response to his
greeting. Folding his newspaper carefully, he laid it on
the chair behind him.

'Is something wrong?' he asked, and Helen thought
she detected a note of resignation in his voice, as if he
could guess what was to come. 'You have that look,' he
went on, half-chiding, 'as if you are being determinedly
aggressive; as you have so often been towards me. Are
you?'

Helen flushed. Her hands were clenched tightly and
she wished she did not feel so much like crying; she
would so much rather have been in his arms instead of
berating him for making unannounced arrangements
for terminating her job with him. 'Don't you think I
have cause to be?' she demanded throatily. 'Don't you
think it would have been more ethical, more—more
fair, to have told me that you were sending Isabella to
school and I wouldn't be wanted for much longer?
Didn't it occur to you that I have to find another job
when I leave here? That the more warning I have, the
more chance I have to—to look around!'

It was so easy to see the way his expression changed
now that she knew that dark, strong face so well, and
Helen had never regretted anything as much as she did
the sudden tightening of his mouth and the change
from warmth to glittering resentment in the black eyes.
'Vincenzo told you,' he said, without even pretending it
was a question, and she nodded without saying anything. 'When? Last night in the garden?' He gave her
barely time to nod assent once more. 'You surprise me!'
he remarked with crushing harshness. 'I would have

credited Vincenzo with taking better advantage of a walk in a moonlit garden with a lovely girl!'

'Not with *me*!' She spoke quickly, breathlessly, and there was a haziness in her hazel eyes that made them shimmer like the topaz Vincenzo had bought her. 'There's nothing between me and Vincenzo, and no matter what you believe, there never was—not in the way you mean!'

Guido's black eyes held hers steadily and she could feel her whole body trembling with emotions she found alarmingly hard to check. 'You speak only for yourself, if you believe that, *mia ragazza*!' he said. 'Do you think I do not know my own brother?'

'Vincenzo is a flirt! I know it and I treated him accordingly, but there was never anything remotely serious between us—now or ever!'

'He did not ask you to go to Australia with him?'

The long lean body seemed to be tensed, and his big brown hands were thrust quickly into his pockets while he watched her, as if he feared they might betray how anxious he was to hear her reply. 'Of course not!' Helen denied quickly. 'Vincenzo knows better than to suppose I'd go! He—he made a joke about it and I told him I couldn't go anyway because I still had a job educating Isabella.' She shook her head, fighting hard against encroaching tears. 'That was when he told me I was going to lose my job very soon; something *you* should have told me!'

'Helen——'

'You could have told me you were—you were getting rid of me!' she insisted, blindly accusing because she could already anticipate the heartache it was going to mean when she never saw him again. She could not stay close to him for much longer either without giving herself away—he knew women too well. 'You never really trusted me, did you, Guido? Ever since that first morning when you accused me of being Vincenzo's mistress, you've questioned my motives—even that wretched necklace—Guido!'

Her anguished cry followed him as he walked away from her, a taut lean figure that moved with such smoothly menacing strides across the big *salotto*, and she winced when he slammed the door behind him without a backward glance. Giving way to tears at last, she watched the door still through the hazy blur until she was sure he wasn't coming back.

It was already over. He would never forgive her for that wild outburst, nor would he understand the helpless fury behind it, and for the first time in her life Helen gave way to utter despair. Curled up in the chair he had just vacated, she buried her face in her arms and wept.

CHAPTER NINE

HELEN was never quite sure how she got through the rest of that day, and she did so quite unaware of the number of times Isabella glanced across at her with dark anxious eyes, puzzled by her obvious unhappiness. Somehow Helen went through the motions of normality, but she did so in a kind of daze, and by the end of the day she had more or less convinced herself that Guido's reason for wanting to get rid of her was because he was beginning to realise how she felt about him. He probably wished to save them both from embarrassment.

Maybe she should have been grateful to him in one way for not prolonging a situation that she had known all along could so easily bring her heartache eventually. But she was too completely overcome at the moment by the realisation that very soon she would be leaving and would never see him again, unless it was by some freak of chance.

She had done her best to disguise the signs of weeping, but had not been altogether successful, and Isabella was unlikely to be the only one to notice, though no one mentioned it, not even Vincenzo. In fact Vincenzo's normally extrovert good humour was markedly subdued, suggesting that Guido had expressed his disapproval in no uncertain terms.

Helen missed lunch and ate very little at dinner that evening, and the moment she had the opportunity she went in search of some books she needed from the schoolroom. The room struck her as chilly and she shivered as she switched on just one of the overhead lights to see her way. It wasn't really cold, but she seemed to have felt chilled all day, and she shrugged her shoulders under the light wool dress she wore.

It was long-sleeved and the colour of cinnamon, a shade that deepened the colour of her eyes and added richness to her light golden hair, while the clinging softness of the material followed her gentle curves enticingly. She knew it suited her without seeing herself reflected in the french windows, and she was in no mood to admire herself at the moment, though she did pause and press her forehead to the chill glass for a second before picking up her books.

Part of the room was reflected behind her, and she lifted her head in sudden alertness when the door opened, watching with anxious eyes to see who had come in search of her. Her heart thudded hard, almost deafening her, when she realised it was Guido who stood just inside the door for a moment before turning to close it behind him, and she swung round quickly, her eyes wide and wary.

Without doubt he had followed her there, for he would have no other reason for coming to the schoolroom at that hour of the day, and he seemed to loom incredibly large in the half-light. Possibly because of her present situation, Helen felt small and somehow shrunken, unlike her normal self and much less confident.

He said nothing for a moment, but stood near Isabella's desk looking at Helen, and as always she noticed every single detail about him, as if they were printed indelibly on her mind. He invariably dispensed with the formality of a tie as soon as the evening meal was over, and her eyes lighted instinctively on that small rapid pulse at the base of his throat, as they always did.

A light grey suit emphasised the lean lines of his body, just as a cream shirt emphasised the bronzed texture of his skin, and he had that curiously menacing air about him that sometimes alarmed her, but always affected her. He had one hand in the pocket of his jacket and his black eyes regarded her with an intensity she found hard to bear, so that she moistened her lips anxiously with the tip of her tongue.

'Guido?'

He so often forced her into making the first move by simply looking at her, and since he seemed disinclined to go to her, she moved from the window and came towards him. But even when she got closer it was impossible to guess what had made him come looking for her. He took note of the flush in her cheeks and the still slightly puffed and evasive eyes, but he did nothing at the moment to put her at ease.

'You have been crying,' he said, as if he had only just become aware of the fact, and the suggestion of regret in his voice caught at her breath.

Helen shook her head, not to deny that she had been crying, but to deny him the right to question her about it. 'I'm all right,' she insisted huskily.

'Is it because you do not want to leave here?'

How could she answer him? Helen thought desperately. He must know she did not want to leave, but she prayed he would not guess just how agonising it was to try and face the thought of a future in which he would have no part. When she did not reply he made another guess, though not in anger; in the deep voice that she always found so affecting.

'Or perhaps it is because I did not tell you before Vincenzo did about sending Isabella to school.' When she still did not say anything, he reached out and lightly touched her cheek, speaking so softly that a little shiver slipped along her spine suddenly. 'Oh, Helen, how foolish you are, *piccina*!'

However gentle his scorn it was just the kind of stimulus her flagging spirit needed, and she lifted her head and looked at him with the first signs of reviving animation in her eyes. 'I suppose it does seem silly to you,' she reproached him, 'but I'm not used to hearing second-hand that I'm being sent packing!'

Helen had seldom seen laughter in his eyes, but it glowed there unmistakably in that moment, and in the circumstances she almost hated him for it. It suggested more definitely that hint of cruelty she had noticed at their first meeting, and she refused to see him as deliberately cruel.

'Were you ever sent packing before?' he asked. 'I was under the impression that this was only your second post since you left training college; and you resigned from the first, I believe, before you were actually—dispensed with.'

She hated feeling childish and his gentle taunting did just that, so that she once again gave him that long reproachful look. 'It doesn't matter,' she insisted. 'You should have——'

'Told you myself. Yes, yes, I know that is what is making you so angry, Helen, but you have not taken into account the fact that Vincenzo—what I believe you call jumped the gun.'

'Whether he did or not, I don't see that it alters anything,' Helen told him, and chanced another brief glance at his face.

The strong arrogant face of a Roman tyrant, she had decided on first acquaintance, but it was now the dearest face in the world to her, even though it hinted faintly of mockery, and the mockery was aimed at her. It was so difficult not to remember the thrill of being in his arms, and the hard, exciting assault of his mouth on hers, and remembering brought an irrepressible thrill of excitement.

'You believe that it is all settled and that I simply did not trouble to tell you?' he suggested. 'My dear girl, not even Isabella knows of it yet! It is an idea that Vincenzo and I discussed, and I conceded was worth trying, that is all. You had no reason to reproach me so bit-

terly and if I was angry, as I *was*—I had reason to be!
In a very short space of time you have suggested that I
am not only immoral but insensitive as well, and I
resent both implications! *Dio mio*, I cannot think what
I have done to deserve such a reputation!'

Helen felt suddenly very small and confused, but she
fought defensively against what he made sound like a
very one-sided case of misjudgment. 'I haven't said you
were either immoral or insensitive,' she denied in a
shaky voice. 'I—I've enjoyed being here and I've never
had any complaints about you as an employer——'

'*Never?*' Guido taunted, and she caught at her bottom lip hastily.

She would not have thought herself capable of crying any more after that furious bout of weeping earlier,
but she again felt alarmingly close to tears, and she did
not want him to see it. 'Is that why you came in here
after me?' she asked in a small unsteady voice. 'To let
me know how I'd misjudged you and to—to put me
firmly in my place yet again? You needn't have
bothered, Guido, I'm well and truly aware of it by
now!'

She half expected he would grow angry, but instead
he looked at her for a moment without speaking, then
reached inside his jacket and took out a square flat box
which he put down on Isabella's desk between them. 'I
came because there were things I wanted to say to you,'
he told her, his voice quiet and restrained. 'Not to—to
verbally chastise you as you seem to think, but to—
explain certain things that I think you should know.'

Helen's hands were trembling and she clasped them
tightly together to try and stop it while she looked at
the black leather gem case on the desk. There was a
scroll of half-erased gold leaf on the lid and she
thought she knew what was in it. 'The Tears of Venus,'
she guessed, and Guido nodded.

'Open it, Helen.'

She shook her head instinctively. 'I'd—I'd rather not.'

Guido leaned past her and raised the lid with long, impatient fingers, and the necklace was revealed, lying like a circlet of frozen raindrops on black velvet, winking and gleaming and reminding Helen of the last time she had seen it. Then it had been lying on the desk in Guido's office, hard and glittering as Olivia Alessio's eyes when she accused her of stealing it, and Helen shivered.

'You do not like it.'

He spoke without bothering to consult her for her opinion, but Helen did not attempt to disagree, because it was true. For all its beauty, the necklace repelled her, if only for its associations. 'I don't like it,' she concurred, then sought to qualify her dislike. 'I suppose because I've never seen it except when there's been some kind of—upheaval concerning it. To me it seems like a—a jinx.'

Guido remained unmoved by her opinion of his family's heirloom, it seemed, for he showed no sign of resenting it. 'I am of a mind to sell it,' he told her, and Helen stared at him blankly. 'It is hardly old enough to be treasured as an heirloom and I have always considered it an ill-omen to the women who owned it, so it seems to me that its value will serve a better purpose. However, *you* shall decide its fate, Helen.'

'Me?' Helen stared at him open-mouthed. 'Oh no, Guido, you can't be serious! How on earth can *I* take the responsibility of deciding a matter like that?'

'Perhaps if you will allow me to go on with what I have to say, you will see how you can take the responsibility, *piccola*. Listen to all I have to tell you and then decide.'

Shaking like a leaf, Helen heard only part of what he was saying, for she could not under any circumstances see herself having the nerve to dictate the eventual fate of the Tears of Venus, and she could not imagine what possessed Guido to come up with such an idea. Ignoring his advice to listen before she made a decision, she spoke up quickly before he began.

'Guido, it's impossible. You can't expect me to——'

Her voice faded under the firm pressure of his mouth and the pressure of his long fingers beneath the hair on her neck sent a myriad tiny shivers thrilling through her body. 'Have I not said that I find that an excellent way of silencing a woman when she is talking nonsense?' he asked, and lightly brushed his lips once more against hers. 'Now listen to me, Helen, for what I have to say is important.'

The fingers under her hair pressed hard for a second and made her tip back her head, and she breathed her assent through parted lips. 'Yes; yes, I'll listen.'

Having gained her attention he withdrew his hands, and instead thrust them into the pockets of his trousers. He also moved away slightly, as if he found it easier to say what he had to say when he was not actually looking at her. 'First there is Isabella.' Helen looked up at him swiftly, but he did not meet her eyes. 'You once suggested that I had fathered Isabella without the formality of marrying her mother,' he went on, 'and it is an impression I cannot blame you for, for it is one that has been deliberately fostered for the past ten years and one shared by most of my family.'

Helen stared at him, trying to bring her racing thoughts under control. Coming so soon after his insistence that she decide the fate of the necklace it was almost too much to grasp. 'Guido, what—what are you saying?'

'I am saying that I am not Isabella's natural father!' he confirmed in a brisk hard voice that she knew stemmed more from anxiety than impatience in this instance. 'But on that I must swear you to secrecy,

Helen; you must promise me never to betray it to anyone!'

'Of course.'

She felt oddly relieved without for the moment realising why it was, but to Guido, it seemed, the rest of his discourse was harder to reveal, for he moved across to stand by the window, in the spot she had been standing herself when he came in. And his back was to her, his gaze on the dim reflection of the room in the glass.

'Did you know that Vincenzo went to an English school?' he asked, and Helen nodded.

'He told me right at the beginning.'

'And you will know, of course, what an appetite he has for pretty girls. Not that I can condemn him for inheriting a trait that we all three get from our father.' A light shrug of his broad shoulders added meaning to the simple admission and reminded Helen of Isabella's insistence that her father liked beautiful ladies.

'I gathered that from something Isabella's said,' she told him, but did not go into details at the moment, merely avoided the black gaze that watched her via the window.

'So?' He thrust his hands into his pockets again and resumed his narrative. 'Vincenzo was barely sixteen when he had his first serious affair. She worked at the school he attended and she was about a year older than Vincenzo, but I am not saying that to excuse Vincenzo, I believe there was genuine affection between them, for a while at least. She was very near her time when I went to England for a four-day event, and Vincenzo was concerned because he had not seen her for several months; he really did care for her enough to worry because they had not quarrelled or taken leave of one another as if they were not to meet again.'

'Vincenzo isn't callous,' Helen interposed, and he gave her a brief look through the mirroring glass.

'It was the old story,' he went on, in the same quiet and oddly flat voice. 'Her parents were too proud of their respectability to want anything to do with her or her child, and she was in a home for unmarried mothers when I found her. Marriage was out of the question, Vincenzo was still a schoolboy and to have broken into his education could have been ruinous. Also, being the youngest son, he was the favourite of both Violante and my father, but the *bambina* had to have someone to care for her and who would be surprised that some-one like me had been——careless? Vincenzo was too fear-ful to argue, and relieved!'

'So you let everyone think you were the father!'

Helen felt a curious stirring in her breast that she had never experienced before, and the need to be near him was irresistible. Walking across, she stood by him, her hands reaching out to touch him; just to touch him before her heart burst from her body and she died for love of him. It was a shattering, head-spinning ex-perience and she could do nothing to hide how she felt, even had she tried.

'Oh, Guido!'

She spoke softly, and he lifted his head for a moment while the black eyes lingered on her reflection. 'She died only a few days after Isabella was born,' he told her in a gentler voice. 'I promised her that Isabella should learn English as well as Italian, and that she would become my daughter, just as if she was my own flesh and blood. By then she cared only for her child, and the promise was all she needed to satisfy her.'

Helen knew she would have loved him whatever he had done, even if Isabella had been his natural child, but to realise how much he had taken on and for how long gave her an agonising need to love him physically as well as in her heart. She ached to enfold his long lean body in her arms and let him know how much she loved him.

He held her reflected gaze for a long moment before he turned and faced her, and Helen looked up at him with eyes that could no longer conceal her feeling for him. 'You realise now why she has not been to school, but been tutored at home?' he asked, and Helen shook her head. It was impossible to think about anything but her love for him, and he shook his head over her slowness while one finger lifted a tendril of hair from her neck and twined it round and round. 'She is Violante's grandchild,' he explained, 'and Vincenzo's daughter. She is—excitable, over-excitable sometimes, and for a long time I feared for her, so that I kept her at home always. But now——'

'Isabella is a perfectly normal and delightful little girl,' Helen told him, though she was reminded of her own thoughts on Isabella's inclination to get over-excited. 'She's highly strung and a little excitable, but that's all. You have nothing to fear by sending her to school, Guido, and she'll love it among other children.'

'The scheme has your approval, then?' She glanced up quickly and saw a glimmer of the old challenging light in his eyes.

'According to Vincenzo you know it's something I've always advocated for her,' she told him.

'Even if it means you get dismissed?'

She dared not look at him when she answered that, for it had become even more unthinkable in the past few minutes, the idea of leaving him for good. 'Even if it means I get dismissed,' she agreed, and tried to keep her voice steady. 'I'm—I'm flattered that you trusted me enough to tell me the truth about her, Guido.'

'How could I not?' he asked, and Helen's cheeks glowed under the steady black gaze. 'One day she will be told; when she is older and better able to understand and accept the truth.'

'She loves you, you need never doubt that.' Helen reached for his hand impulsively, pressing her own slim fingers into the ones that were twined in her hair. She stayed with the matter of Isabella only because it was his wish, for herself she was deeply immersed in more personal and intimate feelings. 'She loves Vincenzo too, but not in the same way; it's you she turns to when she's frightened and in need of reassurance.'

'But she needs a mother.'

Helen felt a sharp stab when her heart lurched in her breast and threatened her breathing, but somehow she steadied her voice. 'Of course she does,' she agreed. 'All little girls need a mother.'

'So!' The now familiar and sometimes infuriating comment gave nothing away as always, and Helen felt suddenly too tremblingly unsteady to stand. Glancing across at the desk where the Tears of Venus still lay gleaming like white fire on their bed of black velvet, he inclined his head jerkily. 'You must decide what is to be done with the Tears of Venus,' he told her, and again Helen's heart felt on the verge of stopping altogether.

'Guido——'

'It is by tradition the property of the eldest son's wife,' he went on without heeding her brief appeal, 'and since I wish to marry you it is your privilege to decide whether or not it shall be sold.' He put his two hands to her cheeks and cupped her flushed face, speaking so softly it was almost a whisper and his lips were only a breath away. 'You have to make up your mind, Helen!'

'Oh, Guido, I——' It was as if the floodgates had opened up and every dream she had ever had suddenly became possible. Her whole body was fired with those fierce, wild emotions that she had sometimes felt were almost too violent. But when she put a hand to touch the vee of bronzed flesh where his shirt opened she gave them free rein, touching a fingertip to the irresistible pulse that beat in his throat. 'Guido, you must know how I feel, I——'

'There is one more thing you should know,' Guido interrupted, but she shook her head quickly.

'No, no, I don't care what else you tell me, it won't make any difference!'

'This will, I think,' he told her, and his long fingers gently opened the neck of her dress, then slid around her neck, stroking her shoulders under the warmth of the material. 'I love you, Helen—my lovely little Helen. *Mia bella bambina, ti amo.*' He stroked down her neck and bent to kiss the soft skin below her ear. 'I have loved you from the moment I saw you on the stairs that first evening. So very young and lovely, and so very determined to fight me every inch of the way on everything and anything!'

'I hated fighting with you,' she breathed the words softly and her eyes were half closed, her skin warming to the hands that drew open her dress until the soft fluttering swell of her breasts betrayed how rapidly she breathed, and the pulsing urgency of her heartbeat.

He touched the pale tender skin lightly with his lips, and she shivered. 'Will you still fight me, *diletta?*' he whispered. 'Or will you let me love you?'

He sat back on the edge of her desk and clasped his hands in the small of her back, drawing her close while his black eyes gleamed darkly, making promises Helen had never dared dream of. The top few buttons of his shirt were already undone and her trembling fingers opened the rest to his waist, stroking over the long, fading scar that ran diagonally across his broad chest.

'I want you to love me!' she murmured. 'I want it more than anything in the world, Guido!' Her mouth to the throbbing pulse in his throat, she pressed her body close so that her soft skin flinched briefly at the brush of dark hair. 'I love you! I loved you desperately while you were scolding me, and even while I

thought Violante was your wife, I couldn't help myself!
I think I've loved you ever since—ever since poor
Violante came into my room and you almost kissed
me!'

'The room that used to be her children's nursery,'
Guido explained, and so solved another mystery.

'Is that why she came? I couldn't understand why
she chose my room instead of one of the others.'

Guido did not answer. Instead he caressed every soft
curve of her body with gentle firm hands, turning his
head to kiss the smooth skin of her inner arm when she
put her hands to comb through the thick black hair
above his ears. Discovering traces of silver in the sable
thickness, she was intrigued and smiled. Then she
raised her parted lips to his and he took them with the
same fierce hunger he had that first time at Santa
Caterina.

But now there was nothing to fear, he would not be
apologising this time and making the excuse that tradition demanded he kiss her, and she responded eagerly
and with no trace of reticence; she loved him. Only for
a moment, when he freed her tingling mouth for a
second or two, did she question him, and she smiled
when she looked up at him with gleaming topaz eyes,
because the answer was not really important.

'Suppose someone comes in,' she murmured.

'No one will,' Guido assured her with a touch of arrogance, and his lower lip was already pursed invit-
ingly. 'I have locked the door, I had no intention of
anyone disturbing us or of you escaping me! Tonight
you are mine, *diletta mia*, and I do not yield you to
anyone! Not tonight or any night!'

With not the slightest inclination to argue the point,
Helen raised her mouth to be kissed again, and over on
the far side of the room the Tears of Venus seemed to
shine just a little less brilliantly. Helen had already decided their fate.

The **HARLEQUIN CLASSIC LIBRARY**
is offering some of the best in romance
fiction—great old classics from our early
publishing lists.

On the following page is a coupon with which
you may order any or all of these titles. If you
order all nine, you will receive a free book—*Meet
the Warrens*, a heartwarming classic romance by
Lucy Agnes Hancock.

The first nine novels in the

HARLEQUIN CLASSIC LIBRARY

1 **Do Something Dangerous** Elizabeth Hoy
2 **Queen's Counsel** Alex Stuart
3 **On the Air** Mary Burchell
4 **Doctor Memsahib** Juliet Shore
5 **Castle in Corsica** Anne Weale
6 **So Dear to My Heart** Susan Barrie
7 **Cameron of Gare** Jean S. MacLeod
8 **Doctor Sara Comes Home** Elizabeth Houghton
9 **Summer Lightning** Jill Tahourdin

Great old favorites...
Harlequin Classic Library
Complete and mail this coupon today!

Harlequin Reader Service

In U.S.A.
MPO Box 707
Niagara Falls, N.Y. 14302

In Canada
649 Ontario St.
Stratford, Ontario, N5A 6W2

Please send me the following novels from the Harlequin Classic Library.
I am enclosing my check or money order for $1.25 for each novel ordered,
plus 59¢ to cover postage and handling. If I order all nine titles, I will receive
a free book, *Meet the Warrens,* by Lucy Agnes Hancock.

- ☐ 1
- ☐ 2
- ☐ 3
- ☐ 4
- ☐ 5
- ☐ 6
- ☐ 7
- ☐ 8
- ☐ 9

Number of novels checked @ $1.25 each = $ _____

N.Y. State residents add appropriate sales tax $ _____

Postage and handling $ _____ .59

TOTAL $ _____

I enclose _____
(Please send check or money order. We cannot be responsible for cash sent
through the mail.)
Prices subject to change without notice.

Name _____
(Please Print)

Address _____

City _____

State/Prov. _____

Zip/Postal Code _____

Offer expires December 31, 1980.   0065633